Discovered!

"This is the police!" a voice boomed. "We have the building surrounded! Drop your weapons and come out with your hands up!"

Karel's reaction was immediate. He snatched up the artefact from the cooling corpse of his guardsman and back-pedalled toward the gate dragging Alex with him. She struggled and kicked, but Karel's arm around her throat was immoveable. Before Douglas could think to intervene, they were through the gate and gone.

"Alex!" Michael shouted in dismay.

Rune Gate

by

Mark E. Cooper

Published by Impulse Books UK

Published by Impulse Books UK November 2012
http://www.impulsebooks.co.uk

Books are available at quantity discounts. For more information
please write to Impulse Books UK, 18 Lampits Hill Avenue,
Corringham, Essex SS177NY, United Kingdom.

Cover design: Ravven -------- www.ravven.com

A CIP catalogue record for this book
is available from the British Library.

ISBN: 978-1-905380-37-4

Printed and bound in Great Britain
Impulse Books UK

Acknowledgments

Special thanks go to Sylverre, Terri, Anne, Scott, Arlene, Sharon, Star, Rob, Erick, Lindi, and all the others hanging out at my favourite writing group. Last but not least, I want to thank Dave Milne for reading an early draft of this book.

Thanks everyone.

1~Murder Most Foul

Alexandra Yorke peered pensively through the windscreen into the night beyond. The radio played something cheerful, but Alex hardly noticed. She glanced at the slip of paper on the passenger seat beside her, but the directions were simple and she remembered them well enough.

Drive southwest on Horse Lake Road to the junction, turn south toward Susanville and keep going for five or six miles to Blake's Ranch.

She knew the roads and didn't need a map; she had grown up in Lassen County. Old man Blake's place was something of a landmark, just as hers was. She rounded another curve in the road and the strobing lights of a half dozen police cruisers came into view. The cars all pointed roughly the same way—up a steep embankment. Alex couldn't see anyone to direct her in the dark, but the cruisers' headlights provided a clue. Most of them pointed into the sky where frustrated drivers, unable to mount the embankment, had abandoned the vehicles. Others shone into the wood that Alex assumed was her destination.

Alex pulled her truck, rattling and groaning, off the

highway and onto the hard shoulder. She downshifted, gunned the old engine, and with a roar the truck eased up the slope. The rear tyres fought for traction on wet ground and she feared her truck might join the forlorn looking police cruisers, but it was made of sterner stuff. It gained the height of the embankment, wheels spinning all the way, and eased onto the level ground beyond. She grinned and patted the dash affectionately. Her grin died when she remembered why there were so many police vehicles with their strobing lights still whirling atop their roofs like some kind of funfair ride.

There would be no fun here tonight.

Deputy Jennifer Hale had awoken her in the night and asked her to come out here. That had been less than an hour ago. Jenn wouldn't answer her questions, but that hardly mattered. She knew what it meant being called out like this.

"I should have said no. Why can't I ever say no?"

She knew why. No matter how it scared her, no matter how unwanted this... this *thing* inside her was, it *was* inside her. She couldn't ignore it; she had tried. The result had been far worse than she could possibly have imagined, and she had a very good imagination—unfortunately. No, nightmares or not, Sheriff bloody Edwards or not, she couldn't refuse Jenn the help she needed.

Alex parked her truck as close to the scene as she could. Cops stood all round, staring into the trees in silence, and that wasn't good in her experience. Whatever the trees contained must be bad. No murder was ever good, but there were degrees of bad on the Yorke Scale of Badness. From what she could see, this was going to be about a *nine-point-oh* on the YSB.

"Shit," she muttered and tried to calm herself in readiness for what she was going to see, and go on seeing for the next few nights in her dreams.

She opened the door and stepped into a muddy puddle. *Perfect.* She ignored the cold water flooding into her shoes, and slammed the door of her truck. She always had to slam it to make it stay shut, but this time she wished she'd let Harry take a shot at fixing it the other day. The noise drew everyone's attention. She frantically tried to shut out the voices bombarding her from every side. The hush was unbroken—no one spoke—yet everyone did. In her mind.

She had known what to expect. Their wants, their needs, their dreams and emotions, battered her defences in an unceasing flood. Like a wave at the beach, it crashed down upon her, drowning her, but she was still there. Like a pillar of rock she endured, ever there, ever strong. It came again but with less power this time. She was stone, hard and unyielding. The third time was almost gentle like a brief surge in the tide welcoming her back. She wasn't fooled. She didn't let it touch the real her. She gave it stone. It withdrew into that ocean of background noise that she had lived with since a child of nine had awoken screaming in the night about the bad man. She closed her eyes, took a shuddering breath, and shored up her weakened defences. She was the rock, ever there, ever strong.

She would endure.

"Ma'am?"

Alex opened her eyes to find a baby-faced police officer in a smokey-bear hat watching her. His badge gleamed, and the reflected light flashing in time with the whirling police lights almost mesmerised her. Above his pocket a shiny brass bar tag displayed his name: Meeks.

"No civilians allowed on the scene, ma'am."

Sheriff bloody Edwards and his stupid games. Her hands fisted deep in her coat pockets. "Jenn… I mean Deputy Hale called me. She asked me to come."

Meeks frowned. "Hale called you? Why would she… you're Alex Yorke?"

She nodded.

"I'm sorry, ma'am. I was told not to let you pass. Didn't you get her message?"

She shook her head. "Tomas told you not to let me pass?"

Meeks nodded. "Sheriff Edwards' orders, ma'am."

"Would you let Jenn know I'm here at least, just in case?"

Meeks pursed his lips doubtfully and Alex feared he was about to refuse. That was the excuse she offered herself for what she did next. Even then, she knew it wasn't much of one, and would berate herself later for giving in to temptation. She opened herself to the web and *pushed*. His life thread hummed gently in her mind. Meeks froze for a timeless moment.

"He…" Meeks blinked rapidly as her influence hit him. "I can do that, ma'am. Sure. But I don't think he will let you over there."

Alex's polite smile was barely there. "Thank you, Deputy."

Meeks nodded and with a puzzled frown, he walked away into the trees.

Alex watched him leave, feeling more in control of things and better able to begin what she came here to do. Her eyes surveyed the area, seeing men and women in uniform, but her Sight—the ability that let her perceive things outside most people's awareness—was a different matter. It showed her multi-coloured threads of light connected to the web of life that was the Earth. If she had been interested, she could have followed it into the trees, across the landscape all the way back to the farm where Katy, her cat, lay in attentive silence before the front door awaiting her return. She paused briefly, letting herself sample the threads of those standing nearby, and the thoughts that inevitably came with her tinkering washed over her.

I hate this goddamned waiting…

Edwards couldn't find his butt with both hands. I could've been sheriff if I wanted…

She looks mighty fine…

Alex smiled at the officer when she realised it was her he was thinking of. Compliments were nice even if never voiced aloud.

...for a witch that is. With those eyes and that face, she could have been a model. I've seen worse...

Alex scowled. She didn't like people calling her a witch. *Wicca* was her religion, not witchcraft, but it was her own fault for being nosy. If she hadn't wanted to hear what he thought of her, she shouldn't have been listening. It wasn't his fault that he couldn't shield his public mind—few people could—that's why she had to shield herself from everyone. Murder was an emotive thing. It brought all kinds of thoughts, dreams, and fears out into the open.

All kinds of things.

It's time to tell her I know she's pregnant. I'm going to marry her and I ain't taking no for an answer this time. Oh god, what if she says no? What will I do without her?

Alex moved on, trying to listen only to those thoughts pertaining to the crime. There wasn't much and that surprised her, but it shouldn't have. She already knew that whatever lay among the trees was bad. They were all trying their best not to think about it.

Jenn and Tomas were approaching her through the trees. She had known them too long to mistake their life threads. Jenn was upset. Alex could feel it even from here. Tomas felt cold as he always did these days. He was upset too, but in a different way; he was so cold, he burned. Alex flinched when her probe touched him. She pulled back, trying not to let her shock show on her face, but still hearing his thoughts despite her effort to shut him out.

Stone. A stone wall like the one at the old mill. Thick and strong and unbreakable. What if she can still hear me? The wall. Think about the wall dammit! Stone... stone... stone... stone... stone!

She turned to face Tomas, catching him by surprise, and he crashed to a halt before her. Despite his attempt at shutting her out, she had felt him approaching. His thread snagged those around him, trying to draw them in. Wherever he went, he drew eyes. Call it charisma, call it good looks, it didn't matter. His thread simply attracted others. She could have picked him out of a crowd thousands strong. Out here, it was as easy as breathing.

"Hello, Tomas."

"Alex."

Alex exchanged a nod with Jenn. "I came as soon as you called, Jenn."

Jenn grimaced and glanced at Tomas. "Yeah, thanks. I'm sorry to bring you out like this. I thought you might be able to help us, but..."

"But?"

Tomas glared at Jenn, but shared it with Alex. "But you're going home right now. Jenn called you in without my permission. No civilians allowed, and that goes double and triple for you."

"Tom, she can help!" Jenn protested. It sounded like something she had said more than once tonight. "You know what she can do."

"I don't believe in that shit!" Tomas snarled.

Alex laughed. "Then why are you showing me that wall? I've seen it before, you know. We used to play there as kids."

He paled. "Keep out of my mind!"

Alex shrugged. "I'm not in it. I don't peek, you know that, but if you insist on shouting at me, I can't help hearing it."

"I'm not shouting."

"In your head you are," she said and sighed. She shouldn't have to explain this again. He knew about her abilities as much as anyone did. "If you want to hide from me, just don't think about it. I can't see what you don't want me to see."

Tomas scowled, but he stopped shouting about his damned wall.

It wasn't strictly true that she couldn't see what people didn't want her to see, but it was close enough to the truth to cause her only a twinge of guilt. She never deep scanned, so she could honestly say she only heard what people broadcast publicly to her.

"Fine," Tomas snapped. "You don't peek, but you're still going."

"Okay."

"Okay?" he said suspiciously. "Just okay?"

"Sure. You don't want me here. I don't want me here. Believe me when I say I don't need more nightmares. When the next body turns up, you can call me. Better yet, don't call me. I really don't need another corpse in my head."

Alex turned away, not listening as Jenn tried to reason with him. She climbed into the truck and started the engine then looked over her shoulder, preparing to reverse back to the highway.

Tomas knocked on her window.

Alex revved the engine and started backing. He slapped her window, hard enough to make it rattle in the frame. Damn, she should have moved faster. She rolled the window down still revving the engine in annoyance.

"Alex, I don't want you here—"

She revved the engine again.

"—you don't want to see it, believe me!" Tomas shouted over the noise.

"I can't hear you!" she yelled, revving the engine again.

"Turn the damn motor off!"

"*What?*"

Tomas reached through the window for the keys and the motor died. "I said turn that damn thing off and listen to me! You haven't changed at all have you? All this time in the big city and you're still the arrogant little bitch you always were. You still think the world can't touch you. Well you're wrong, dammit!"

"You finished?" Alex said coldly and reached for the keys.

Tomas grabbed her hand.

She flinched, trying to block him out, but the contact

created a bridge between them. She saw a face crying tears of blood, a huge tree looming over her in the shadows, and blood… so much blood on the ground. Worse than those grisly and disjointed images, she saw again the night she told him what she was, what she could do. She saw again his fear and felt her despair when he rejected her. Tomas' face paled as he relived that night with her.

Alex wrenched her hand free. "*Don't touch me!*" she screamed. "*Don't ever touch me!*" She panted, her senses reeling. Tomas had breached her defences so easily it left her dizzy and sick. She forced her thoughts back to the pillar of rock. Tomas' thoughts slammed against it, but she was stone—hard and unyielding. Ever there, ever strong. "Don't ever touch me again," she whispered.

"My god. That was… you were…" Tomas took a deep breath and stilled his shaking. "What's happened to you? It's gotten worse, hasn't it?"

"What would you know about it?" she said, spitting the words in his face.

Tomas' face darkened. "Nothing. Only that never happened when we… when we made love."

"Didn't it? I can't remember."

His lips tightened and he looked away, unable to meet her eyes.

She felt warmed and savagely pleased by his reaction. She wanted him hurt. If there were any justice in the world, her lie would have hurt him as much as he had hurt her. He broke her heart all those years ago, broke it so badly she had been celibate ever since, not daring to risk herself again.

Tomas sighed and muttered something under his breath. "I didn't want you here, Alex. I still don't, but Jenn's right. I do need you. I hate it, but I need what you can do."

Alex squeezed her eyes shut. She should leave. She was unsettled and his touch had weakened her defences. She should leave, but she knew she wouldn't. The next one to die would be her fault if she didn't do all she could here. She reached to open the door, but Tomas opened it for her. She stepped out of the truck and found herself being watched again, all eyes were turned her way. They had heard her scream at their sheriff, and although they didn't know what it was about, they were speculating freely. She shook her head tiredly when she realised that most of them thought it was a lover's quarrel. Sometimes it felt like everyone in the county knew they had once been an item.

"It's this way," Tomas said, reaching for her arm.

Alex flinched back and nearly fell in her haste to get away.

Tomas lowered his hand slowly to his side. She sidestepped him and made for the tree line. There was a short silence and then two pairs of feet following—Jenn and Tomas.

Alex walked into the trees a short way, then turned to her friend. "You know, Jenn, I was surprised when you told me where to meet you."

Jenn cocked her head to one side. "Why?"

"Aren't we out of your jurisdiction?"

Jenn shook her head.

"We have joint jurisdiction with State," Tomas said. "Have done for two years now. Alice… the Mayor helped push it through."

"Yeah?"

Tomas nodded. "A lot's happened since you've been gone, Alex. Anyway, Blake called us so this one's all ours. I have to keep the staties informed, but that's no hardship. I just fax a report once a week and they do the same for me about their cases. It works. If I need their help on something or vice-versa there's always the phone."

"Sounds refreshing," Alex said mockingly.

Tomas frowned. "Refreshing?"

"No pissing contests."

Jenn chuckled, but sobered quickly. "We got the call a couple of hours ago. Old man Blake said he saw a light through the trees. Thought it might be a trespasser. You know how he is."

Alex nodded. "A couple of hours and you're still out here?"

Jenn shrugged. "I couldn't find anything at first."

"You were the first on scene?"

"Yeah. I talked to Blake to see what he knew, and then came out here to check his fences. It was so dark that I didn't expect to find anything. Blake said he saw a light in the trees, but it was gone when I got here. I scouted around and found… it."

"Man or woman?" Alex asked, stepping carefully over tree roots.

"Woman," Jenn said using a tree to steady herself as she navigated the same roots.

"Anyone missing from town?"

"Thank god, no," Tomas said like a prayer. "She's not local, just passing through would be my guess. I have someone checking the motels and guesthouses. We won't know much until tomorrow or the next day."

Alex pursed her lips. Nothing they had said told her why she was here. "I don't usually get called in unless something is seriously weird…" She stopped when she saw it. "Oh."

"Yeah," they said together.

Alex had been wrong. This went way beyond nine-point-oh on the YSB. It might be time to raise the upper limit again because this was a ten on anyone's scale. The woman had been bound naked to a tree. That was bad enough, but what had been done to her was nothing short of weird; sick as well, but weird.

Alex clamped a fist of iron around her emotions and clinically studied the scene. She noted the body bag and stretcher waiting to receive the victim. Two EMTs waited nearby. Their eyes wandered toward the tree then drifted guiltily away. They made Alex angry just being here, witness to the woman's degradation. It wasn't their fault that they were here. Alex was sure they didn't want to be, but still it made her angry. No one had cut the poor thing down, and that was her fault for taking so long in coming.

"Has anyone touched her?" she asked, the pity she tried to hide was evident in her hushed voice.

Jenn shook her head. "I kept everyone away, Alex. I didn't need to check for a pulse."

"No, I don't suppose so," Alex agreed.

A photographer stood with the EMTs. No doubt he had already performed his job by recording everything in all its gory detail. A little to one side two women stood with a man all wearing white coveralls. She knew who they were—CSI. They glared at Alex, looking really pissed. Jenn or Tomas—she was betting on Jenn—had kept them off the scene. Their equipment remained unused at their feet. The team leader was a man she knew only slightly. Eric Radford; he didn't like her much, but that was okay. She didn't like him either.

"Sheriff!" Radford stomped angrily toward them, but Tomas raised a hand and Radford halted at a distance, scowling. "You're risking this entire investigation! Evidence is being destroyed while my team cools its heels waiting for this… *charlatan* to do her mumbo jumbo!"

"Charlatan?" Alex said with a sweet smile. "I thought I was a witch."

"Alex, shut up," Tomas said in a tired voice. "This won't take five minutes, Eric. You can bear with me for that long, can't you?"

Radford's face reddened. "Have I got a choice?"

"No actually." Tomas turned away and ushered Alex along.

"I'll be watching!" Radford yelled at their backs. "It's all going in my report!"

Tomas sighed. "I guess I'll have another visit from the mayor to look forward to then."

Jenn laughed quietly.

Alex stopped about ten feet from the tree. "Where are her eyes?"

"Can't find 'em. Probably won't until we catch the sick bastard," Tomas grated.

"Trophies?"

Tomas nodded. "That would be my guess. It happens more than you would think. A lot of killers take something from the victim. Not like this, but something; jewellery maybe, or a piece of clothing."

Alex had a degree in criminal psychology, but Tomas had never taken her studies seriously, not even when they were together. She'd had some police training too while living in L.A. On the job training, you might say, but that didn't make her cop enough for him. All serial murders had things in common, like trophy taking. It was premature calling this case part of a serial murder because it was the first one...

Alex frowned. Tomas hadn't wanted to call her in. "This *is* the first one I take it?"

Jenn nodded. "This is the first. Things have been quiet until now."

"Why?" Tomas asked suspiciously. "You know something. What?"

"Whoever did this has killed before," Alex said. It was obvious the moment she saw the victim. "You know the pattern, Tom. A first time murderer almost always kills in the heat of the moment. The murder is unplanned, often triggered by a family argument. The victim is usually the wife or husband of the killer. But this, this was planned. She wasn't killed and dumped here. She was brought here alive then mutilated in a ritualistic way. He's done this before; I guarantee it. He's too good; he knew exactly what he was doing. He had the rope already prepared for tying her to the tree, and her clothes aren't here. He took them with him to hide evidence. That would be my guess."

Alex circled the tree, noting the ropes had been cut neatly

and tied in the same way using a complicated knot that she didn't recognise. The woman had been tortured, but she hadn't bled to death. Alex doubted the killer was merely interested in inflicting pain; he had been working some kind of ritual. He took his victim's heart; probably last of all.

"The heart?" Alex said, searching the ground nearby.

"Not here," Jenn said. "You're thinking, what, some kind of pagan ritual?"

"Witches?" Tomas said eagerly, snatching at any lead that might help.

She flinched. "Not the kind you're thinking of. A practicing Wiccan would be just as horrified by this as we are, probably more so. Wicca is a religion, Tom. It has very little to do with the myths of evil witches casting spells on people."

Tomas scowled at his boots, not arguing but obviously not going to agree either. "Not witches. Satanic then?"

Alex completed her circuit of the tree and stopped to examine some of the cuts on the body. "No, I don't think so. These signs, I haven't seen anything quite like them before, but I feel as if I should know them."

She closed her eyes and reached out with her senses as she circled the tree again. The first thing she noticed was the complete lack of life in the tree. It was dead, yet if she opened her eyes, she would still see green leaves on its branches. It was summer and the forest was green, yet she knew if she came back here in a few days the tree would have bare branches. What could kill a three hundred year old tree overnight? Its roots went deep. She followed its dull and lifeless thread into the ground and gasped at what she found. Its thread had been severed from the web! How? She hadn't known that was possible. Nothing could snap a thread like this, not even death. Death was part of the never-ending cycle of life and therefore part of nature and the web. She stopped in front of the woman and slowly reached out to touch her.

Alex stiffened as the woman's essence flowed into her,

bringing with it a numbing cold and the scent of vanilla. Fragmentary memories flashed before her eyes, and ghostly voices whispered in her ears. Most of all, she felt a terrible sense of loss.

"Alex, are you all right?" Jenn asked.

Her name was Sharon Brydon and she had lived in Leavitt her entire life. She worked behind the counter of the local bar and grill. She was saving her college tuition and planned to major in psychiatry. Her parents were so proud of her and Tony said...

Alex flinched away from Sharon's memories of her boyfriend and family. She needed to come forward to just before her death. She willed herself not to feel anything. She must only be a witness, not a participant. How many times had she drummed that into herself? A hundred, two hundred? No, not that many surely?

She left work later than usual; Bert had asked her to help him cash up. It was well after ten when she pulled her coat on and stepped into the night. Tony would be waiting up for her. She smiled and turned down the alley. She didn't have time to flinch when something struck her in the face.

"My eyes! Oh my eyes!" Alex cried, covering them with her hands. "He threw something in my face. It burns!"

"That's enough!" Tomas yelled. "I said that's enough!"

Her eyes were stinging and burning. Tears poured over her cheeks and her screams turned to muffled whimpers as one of those gloved hands clamped itself over her mouth. A blow to her face stunned her and a moment later, she was forced into a car. A second, much harder blow sent her into oblivion.

Alex tried to move forward. She pushed through Sharon's pain and found the tree. The tree...

She cried out as the men ripped her clothes off and threw her against the tree. She fought against them, trying to keep her hands free but…

"Too tight…" Alex panted and groaned at the pain of Sharon's bruises. "He tied the ropes too tight to pull free."

"Can you see his face?" Tomas asked eagerly. "Can you describe him?"

Radford cursed and shouted something, but Alex ignored him. Sharon's fear filled her until there was nothing but despair. Sharon knew, *had known*, she would die. She had fought hard against that knowledge in the beginning, but deep down she knew that she would never see her Tony again.

"Tony, oh Tony," Alex sobbed. Tears burned her eyes and ran over her cheeks as if they would never stop.

"Tony?" Jenn asked, her pen hovering over a notebook. "Is that his name, Alex?"

She swallowed her sobs and shook her head. "Boyfriend. My boyfriend, I mean Sharon's boyfriend. I love him so much. She loves him, we love him, I…"

A shadow-cloaked figure moved toward her. It was a man, she thought it was a man, but no matter how hard she tried, she could not penetrate the shadows that hid his face from her. A second man watched the Shadowman fearfully. She stilled like a fox in the headlights of an approaching car and willed herself not there. Hopelessness filled her. Oh Tony, will you remember me? Will you remember why you loved me?

Shadowman's lackey backed fearfully away. He turned and bolted into the trees.

She sobbed uncontrollably. Sharon's despair was like the end of the world and Alex's hatred of Shadowman knew no bounds. If she had known where he was right now, she would have stopped at nothing to see him brought down.

She clutched her arms, shivering uncontrollably. Her breath smoked as the temperature plummeted around the tree. There were curses and shouts from the CSI team watching from the wings with frightened eyes.

Her eyes widened in fear as they fixed on something only she could see. "He has a…"

…knife in his left hand and something round like a little wagon wheel in his right. He chants something, making passes over the wheel with the knife. The air thickened all about and she whimpered. The breeze suddenly died. Something slimy and evil poured over her. There was nothing there! Nothing! She could feel it caress her body intimately like ghostly hands made of air.

"Please no, God make him stop. Please let me go… our father, who art in heaven…"

"Foul," Alex choked out thickly. "Unclean thing!" She hissed as if the Shadowman could hear her. She wanted to retch at the taste of his foul magic. "A spell… evil."

"I knew it!" Radford shouted. "Devil worshippers and she's one of them!"

"Shut the fuck up!" Tomas snarled. "Or so help me God, I'll put you away."

"How dare you—"

"Meeks!" Tomas roared at the top of his lungs and Meeks came running with his gun drawn looking for trouble. Tomas pointed at Radford. "Get him out of here until I call for him."

"But… yes sir, Sheriff." Meeks turned to Radford. "Sir, please don't make me force you."

"You haven't heard the last of this, Sheriff," Radford said. "The mayor will have something to say about this!"

"Yeah, whatever," Tomas said tiredly. "She usually does rag on my arse on Mondays."

Meeks led Radford away while the rest of his team watched.

Jenn hovered near Alex, and Tomas joined her. Alex saw it all as if dreaming. Sharon and the Shadowman were more real to her right now.

"Evil," Alex whispered and wrung her hands. The air on her skin felt thick and greasy—evil made manifest. "I'm going to be…"

…sick. Sharon's stomach rebelled and she swallowed, gulping air. Shadowman stopped and pointed the knife at her eyes. She screamed at the tearing agony. She screamed and screamed her throat raw. The last thing she saw was the glint of polished steel plunging toward her face before she entered eternal darkness.

Alex howled silently as a vale of blackness descended over her sight. Surely Sharon would die of the shock, but no, Alex was still with her. Warm sticky fluid flowed from her hollow eye sockets. Evil flowed all around and frost began to form over Sharon's dead body and the tree she was tied against.

Tomas' teeth chattered.

Alex struggled to voice what Sharon was… *had* gone through. "I'm blind and I'm going to die. He killed me, will kill me, did kill me. I beg him not to hurt me, but he just laughs." Alex grunted and doubled over, trying to hold back more screams. "He cuts me—he's left handed. He's murmuring words like a prayer as he cuts. I can't understand what he's saying. He has a very thick accent." She fell to her knees. "He's drawing something on me with the knife, like words but not words, like pictures that mean something. I'm screaming, but no one comes. I'm dying… I'm dead."

Alex's eyes bulged and her breath stopped in her throat as Shadowman thrust the dagger into her chest and began sawing. Her heart stuttered and she took a ragged breath as Sharon rushed away from her. Alex tried desperately to follow. She knew it was foolish to hang on, she would die, but she tried anyway. Sharon raced ahead, out of reach—pulled violently away by an irresistible force. Alex tried to reach her, but Sharon's thread was in tatters. It tore in her grasp and Sharon's sense of self dissolved into a meaningless chaos of broken memories.

Tony... her parents celebrating... Bert smiling at her from behind his counter... a birthday party... I'm five mummy, isn't that great?! Tony... Tony... Tony...

"Wrong," Alex moaned, her throat clogged with grief for the little girl who would be... *was* murdered. "It's wrong. Something's not right. It's not supposed to happen like that."

Jenn stared into her eyes. "Is it something we can use?"

Alex blinked at Jenn vaguely. »I'm dead, but Shadowman still cuts me—I mean Sharon—and mumbles words. I'm dead, she's dead, we're dead... a light, a door opening... Shadowman steps through without looking back. I'm dead..."

Jenn grabbed Alex and shook her. "Come on, Alex. That's enough. Snap out of it."

Alex looked into her friend's face blankly. "I'm dead."

"Wake up!"

"I'm dead."

"Come back, Alex!" Jenn's voice rang with fear. "You're not dead, do you hear me? You're not dead!"

"I'm dead," Alex said one last time and fell into Jenn's arms.

* * *

"Jesus," Tomas whispered under his breath as he watched one of his men drive Alex home. Another followed in her truck.

"Yeah," Jenn said, shaken. "I didn't know it would be like that."

"It never was before. She's getting worse."

Jenn shook her head gently. "Sharon Brydon from Leavitt,

she said. Do you believe it?"

Tomas nodded.

"I'll have someone check her out. See if she's listed as missing. What about that stuff at the end?"

"I don't know, but we didn't find a car. Where the hell is it?"

"You think Alex is right about there being two of them?"

Tomas nodded, still seeing Alex's pale and haunted face. He shivered. "If you believe all of what Alex saw, and I'm not saying I do, then the perp didn't leave by car. That means someone else drove them out here. I want him."

"Maybe Alex will remember more after she's had a rest."

"Maybe."

* * *

2~Questions

Alex patted Smokey on his muscled neck and turned in the saddle to look back at the house. The phone was ringing again. It had been ringing off the damn hook ever since the story broke. The leak could only have come from a small group of people. Jenn and Tom wouldn't have said anything for fear of damaging their chances of prosecuting the killer, so it had to have been the photographer, one of the crime scene investigators, or one of the EMTs. Alex's money was firmly on Radford's CSI team if not Radford himself.

The days following the discovery of Sharon Brydon's remains had been a strain, especially the nights when Alex relived the horror of Sharon's last hours, but she had been through this kind of thing before. She had known what to expect when she agreed to help Jenn, but that didn't make the nightmares less real to her. The dreams would fade eventually, and the pain would grow less, until one day it would become nothing but a disturbing memory. She could live with that. She'd been living with similar things for a lot of years now. She'd had plenty of practice.

Alex urged Smokey into a gallop. "Go, boy!" she shouted urging him to greater speed and away from the phone. "Go!"

Smokey's ears swivelled to listen and he ran even faster.

Alex loved riding. It was a way to let go and not think about things for a while. Smokey's thoughts were simple, full of the joy of bunching muscles and the turf beneath his hooves. They were no threat; she could let herself become one with him without fear. With a shift of her weight, she turned him to follow the trail he knew so well. He hardly needed even that small guidance. They were one. A few minutes into the run however, she slowed and dismounted when she found a break in the fence bordering her property.

"Bloody wind." She sighed, eyeing the fresh wound on the tree nearby. A branch had fallen, breaking the top rail.

She pushed and pulled until the branch came free. She shoved it off the fence, but the rail was beyond repair. It was broken in three pieces. It was no big thing, she only needed a new rail and a handful of nails to fix it, but that meant going into town to buy supplies. She really didn't feel like going into town, but the fence wouldn't fix itself.

She patted Smokey, trying to decide what to do. Going into Susanville was a risk. The reporters knew she wouldn't give interviews, she had made that plain enough, but that wouldn't stop them from asking their dumb questions. The Chronicle would go on rehashing the story whether she cooperated or not, so she had chosen not.

"Hell," she snarled, feeling as if the world were closing in on her sanctuary.

She glanced at the broken fence again. It was just a fence, but it suddenly seemed full of portent and loomed large in her mind. Her chest felt tight and she started to pant. Go to town or hide here, be brave or be a coward, stay or run. She couldn't run, not again. Where would she go?

Smokey sidestepped as her agitation flooded through him. "Whoa, boy. I'm sorry." She hastily built a wall between them and regretted the loss of peace their connection had lent her. "Let's walk back. I've got to go into town."

Braving people's curiosity, Alex drove into Susanville and parked outside of Miller Brothers. It was the one place sure to have what she needed in stock, and she had an account there. George and Michael Miller were partners in the business that had been in their family since… well, since forever.

George's arthritis was giving him problems again. She could feel the dull but persistent pain in his knees as she entered the store. It was like a buffer between their thoughts and she was grateful for it. He looked up from what he was doing when the bell rang over the door.

"Hey, Alex," George said, stacking a last few tins of wood stain. He grunted and winced as he pushed himself up with a hand on his knee.

"Hey, George, how goes it?"

"Pretty good. I just sold a shit-load of pentachloro-phenol."

Pentachlorawhat? "Yeah? Big congrats."

"Thanks. Michael persuaded me to buy the damn stuff a couple of years back. He worked out a good deal for it, but the buyer pulled out. I never thought I'd see the back of the stuff."

Alex grinned. George sounded disgusted that his brother's purchase had come good even though it meant extra money in his pocket. Michael might be his partner in the business, but he was still his brother. Like brothers everywhere, they were competitive. George was the elder of the two. An ex-marine, he was wide in the shoulders and barrel-chested. Even decades after leaving the corps, she could still easily picture him in his drill sergeant uniform. His posture was still erect, his spine ramrod straight, and his silver hair ruthlessly cut in the style he had worn most of his life.

Alex could tell that Michael wasn't here at the moment. "How is Michael?"

George shrugged. "The same."

"Sorry."

"Nothing to feel sorry about, Alex. He's my brother and I love him, but we both know he can be an idiot sometimes. I'm surprised Anne put up with his straying ways as long as she did."

George might be surprised, but Alex wasn't.

Anne, Michael's long suffering wife, had stayed with him exactly the length of time needed to see both of her kids safe. She had left her husband not a week after her girls moved into their own places and hadn't looked back.

"He's living with you?"

George nodded. "He had to sell his place as part of the settlement. It's fine, really. Martha doesn't mind his company. As long as he doesn't start bad mouthing Anne, that is. Woo boy, the last time he tried she nearly skinned him!"

Alex grinned.

George stepped behind the counter. "So, what can I do you for?"

She handed him a slip of paper with the measurements for the new rail. "I just need the one."

"Hmmm. I've got some pre-treated boards out back, but I'll have to cut one down to suit. Sorry, Alex, but I'll have to charge you for the whole thing. No one will want the off-cut."

Alex shrugged, she could cover the cost. "That's okay. Would you load it in the back of my truck for me? It's just outside. I have another errand to run."

"No problem. I'll have it waiting for you when you get back."

"Thanks, George." She started for the door.

"Alex?"

Here it comes.

Alex tried not to feel the tension building in the muscles of her neck and shoulders. She held the door open, ready to flee into the street, and consciously forced herself to relax. She looked back over her shoulder.

George held her eyes. "It true what they're saying?"

"What who are saying?" she asked warily.

"The Chronicle."

Alex sighed. "What are they saying now?"

"You haven't read it?"

She shook her head.

"I have a copy of it here somewhere."

George went into the back storeroom. Now was the time for her to flee, but she needed the wood. It was surprisingly hard to let go of the door and go back. George reappeared with a copy of the Chronicle and spread it on the counter for her. The headline with her picture below it on the front page was self explanatory.

Witch Called In To Consult On Local Murder.

"Oh," Alex said weakly.

She stared at the photo showing her pale and haunted face looking through the police cruiser's window and wondered where the photographer had hidden. She didn't remember seeing or sensing anyone. The headline and picture were bad enough, but the story was worse. It stirred up old history best forgotten. The mention of Satanists was scaremongering and damned irresponsible. There would be a witch hunt next, and who was the only person around here that everyone agreed was a witch? She swallowed and smiled weakly at George. Her stomach roiled and she suddenly felt hot and cold all over. She took deep breaths, hoping for the sick feeling to pass.

George held her eyes. "Is it true?"

Alex couldn't tell what he thought about it without trying a deep scan. She wouldn't do that. Not to him, not to anyone. All she felt from him was the constant discomfort in his knees and a feeling of curiosity. She was reluctant to give any part of the story substance, but denying it would be a lie. She didn't lie to friends, didn't lie to anyone if she could avoid it. Lies tended to go wrong and bite her on the butt when she was least ready for it.

She sighed. "Yeah, it's true."

"Well, shit. We gotta find the sumbitch and kill his arse!"

Alex's lips twitched into a grin and her mood lightened a little. "You don't care what they're saying about me?"

"The witchy stuff?"

"Yeah."

George smiled. "Nope! Live and let live I say. Besides, I know you about as well as anyone does. You're good people. They can say all they want, they won't change my opinion. And then there's the fact the Sheriff called you in at all. I trust his judgment. He's solid. If he wanted you there, I'm willing to bet he had a damn good reason."

"He did." Alex shivered as she remembered Sharon's bloody face. "He did."

"You reckon the sumbitch is still out there?"

Did she? Alex cocked her head and searched within herself, exploring the part of her that let her see things like Sharon's death. The moment she thought about the *thing*, it surged into her grasp, almost eager to be used. She let it flow out of her and merge with the web. There was a shadow over the town. The web was weakened here because of it, and it wasn't the dominance of steel and stone over growing things either. She knew what that felt like from living in the city. There was something slimy, something *evil* about the shadow. She had seen and felt some awful things in her life, but she had never called anything truly evil until seeing Sharon's death. Shadowman was evil, and so was this shadow. Was it him? What else could it be?

Alex shivered. "Yeah, he's still out there all right."

"That's what I figured," George said grimly. "I'm going to load my damn gun no matter what Martha says. It's no good without bullets now is it?"

"I guess not. You keep a gun here?"

He nodded. "I have one at home too, but Martha won't let me load it. Well, I guess it's time I put my foot down. She can have her way when this is all over and she's safe."

Alex left the store thinking about her own protection. She had a gun at the farm and a permit to carry it, but somehow she didn't think Tomas or his men would like her walking around with it in her pocket. She glanced around feeling suddenly exposed. In L.A. she had carried her gun everywhere. In fact, the police had insisted she do so while working with them. Most times she had stayed in the car, but not always. She was even shot at once, but that was a fluke, and she hadn't needed to shoot back. By the time she remembered she was carrying a gun, it was all over. She wasn't planning on making a habit of coming into town, but just in case, she decided to start carrying it again despite Tomas' disapproval.

The library was quite a walk up Main Street, but George needed her truck for the new rail. It was a nice day, sunny but not too hot. She didn't mind walking. She nodded to those people she knew, smiled politely but absently at those she didn't, and made her way to the library.

Thoughts of the shadow and of the runes she planned to research, were such distractions that she didn't notice people stopping to stare at her as she passed the mall. The background noise of their thoughts should have warned her, but the change from vague ruminations to directed hostility was a gradual one. By the time she noticed a common thread coming to the fore, it was too late to hide. She turned to find people scattered here and there, watching her in silence. They were like little islands of stillness and hostility in the background noise of thoughts bombarding her. Standing amongst so many busy people coming and going, they stood out.

Brazen hussy! Look at her daring us to say something. She probably killed that poor woman for one of her evil spells. Everyone knows the story of how her parents died

in that fire. I bet she did that too. Probably killed them to stop them telling anyone she's a witch...

Alex was so outraged by what she heard, she nearly answered the accusation without thinking. She didn't know who her accuser was. It could have been any one of a number of women watching her. It wasn't a man's mind voice, she could tell that, but picking out her silent accuser from a crowd was hard to do without preparation.

Alex swallowed her anger before it could make her do something she would regret. She couldn't even defend herself with words. If she did, it would lend credence to her accuser's accusations, and everyone would wonder if she were mad. She turned and continued on her way, but it was hard.

She hears voices, that's what they say...

No such thing as witches. They should leave the poor girl alone.

She looks sad...

Probably killed the woman to keep her secret.

How else could she know so much about it? Eric was right there when it happened. He said he saw her go all witchy, babbling about dying and stuff. Weird.

Alex stiffened. Radford *had* blabbed about what he saw; she had a good mind to go and see him about it. She knew a few tricks that would make him damn uncomfortable for a few days. She drew a sharp breath when she realised what she was thinking. To use her power to hurt someone... She shook her head. It went against the Wiccan rede and all she believed in. Alex hurried on with her head down, determined not to make eye contact with anyone from then on.

Feeling better when the hostile thoughts gave way to the usual background noise, she slowed her pace. Up ahead, she found Judith Nielson in her garden. She waved and stopped for a moment.

"Hello, Mrs. Nielson. What are you up to this fine day?"

...they should have some respect. I knew her

grandfather, he wouldn't have put up with any funny business. There's no truth to any of it. Damn newspapers. If I were her, I'd sue them for every cent.

Judith sat back on her heels and looked up at her. "Hello, dear. Just a little weeding. They seem to pop up like magic when I'm not looking."

She should find herself a man. If I'd looked like that at her age I would have been fighting them off with a stick!

Alex coughed and tried not to laugh.

"That sounds nasty. You aren't coming down with a cold are you?"

"I'm fine."

"Glad to hear it," Judith said and hesitated. "Listen dear, you can tell an old busybody like me to go to hell if you want, but can I give you a piece of advice?"

"I wouldn't dream of inflicting you on hell, Mrs. Nielson."

Judith grinned. "I think you need to nip this witch business in the bud. You can't let that rag get away with saying those things about you. If I were you, I'd sue."

Alex sighed and nodded. "I would like to, but you see they didn't actually lie. They stretched things a little, but they didn't lie. My parents *were* killed in a fire and they never did find out what caused it. I *do* live alone and I *was* called to the crime scene to help the sheriff in the night. They didn't actually call me a murderer and I am Wiccan. All they did was bring up my studies and the stuff I did in L.A. for the police."

"But you're not a bad girl, Alex! They make you sound like some kind of... *of weirdo!*"

Alex laughed at the outrage on Judith's face. "A weirdo?" She chuckled again. "I've been called worse things."

Judith gestured up town. "At least go over there and give them your side of the story."

"I can't give them anything. The sheriff would put me behind bars if I told anyone what I shouldn't."

"But the papers have already done that!" Judith said, outraged.

"And I bet the sheriff is after whoever leaked the story too."

"Humph! A fat lot of good that will do your reputation now."

"Don't worry about me, Mrs. Nielson. My friends know me well enough not to believe what they read, and the others don't matter."

Judith sighed. "Just be careful, dear. You would be surprised what foolish people will believe. Superstition can make them do some pretty nasty things."

She was right about that.

"I'll be careful. Don't work too hard," Alex said and walked on.

"I won't," Judith called after her. "Mind you take your own advice!"

Alex waved without looking back.

Upon entering the library, Alex found a vacant terminal and logged on. One of the first things she had done when she moved back to the farm was to rejoin the library. Her studies were important to her, and not just because of what she and the L.A.P.D had done together. The thing inside her was part of her, and yet she didn't understand it. She wanted to understand it more than anything. It was the only way she might learn to get rid of it, or at the least, control it.

Unlike other days, she wasn't here to brush up on criminal psychology and parapsychology, nor was she interested in studying the latest theories regarding psychic abilities and the paranormal. She had something more urgent on her mind. One of the things that still puzzled her was the certainty she had seen symbols like the ones carved into Sharon's body before. They felt familiar, yet she couldn't say why. Was it something from her studies?

She had studied something similar once, in an attempt to

aid the police in catching a killer. The man had been caught eventually, through no effort of hers, and had taken the secret of his bizarre rituals and runes to the grave with him. They haunted her still—those little clay tablets he'd left beside his victims, taunting her with her failure. She shivered. She wouldn't let this case become a repeat of that one. She wouldn't be responsible for any more deaths.

Alex called up the texts she'd used on the case and went in search of them. The library was a good one, but it didn't have the book she most wanted. Luckily it did have the other two, and she was satisfied for now. She sat at an empty table and began work. It was obvious right away that the runes didn't match. She had been so sure that she recognised them, but from where? If it hadn't been in the books she had used back then, where else could it have been?

She snapped upright in her seat and a slowly widening smile replaced the scowl she had been wearing. She remembered where she had seen symbols like those used on Sharon, and it wasn't in a book. It was in an old case file she was given by... She nodded. Agent Freemont had shown it to her. Good old Freemont. He would help.

Alex replaced the books upon the shelves and hurried outside.

When Alex entered the sheriff's office, silence fell with a thud—not literally, but it felt like it to her. She stood in the door, transfixed by a dozen stares. All of them were giving her cop eyes—evaluating her, measuring her, judging and dissecting her. She blocked out their silent evaluations and busied herself with closing the door. It gave her an excuse to break eye contact.

She walked up to the counter that divided the office. "Is he in?"

Conversation slowly picked up again.

Deputy Chase leaned his elbows on the counter. "Sheriff

Edwards is in a meeting. Can I help?"

"I'm not sure. I just remembered where else I've seen symbols like those cut into Sharon Brydon."

Chase jerked upright and looked around for eavesdroppers, and then hunched forward again. "Where?"

Alex leaned forward to mirror Chase. "Well, that's the problem. Tom... Sheriff Edwards wouldn't like me telling just anyone. I thought I better tell him in person. Do you think he would be interested?"

"I'm sure he would, ma'am."

"Well then?"

"Ma'am?"

Alex smiled. "Don't you think you should tell him I'm here?"

Chase nodded quickly and left. A few moments later, he stuck his head out of an office and gestured for her to come ahead. She lifted the flap in the counter expecting to be reprimanded any moment, but no one took any notice of her. She followed the corridor and stepped into Tom's office. He wasn't alone.

"You can go back to the desk, Neil," Tomas said.

Chase's face fell. "Ah hell, I knew you were gonna say that."

"I'm sure you'll hear all about it later," Alex said with a grin. Chase rolled his eyes and closed the door quietly behind him. She turned her attention to the other person present. "Hello, Mayor. I hope I'm not intruding."

Mayor Alice Polson smiled. "You know you are, Alex, but I'm sure you won't let that worry you."

Tomas shook his head. "Never did before."

Don't piss her off, Alex. Please don't piss her off. I've just got her seeing things my way. Don't give her an excuse to change her mind...

Alex wondered what he meant by getting the mayor to see things his way. Did it have anything to do with her? Probably not. She shut out his thoughts and concentrated briefly on the mayor, hoping for enlightenment. Alice was unhappy with Alan Walsh, the editor for the Chronicle. He had done something he had promised not to do. Whatever it was, it had put the mayor in a bad position. That's why she was here.

That bastard promised me! He promised to keep the voodoo angle out of this, and then he pulls a stunt like that? I'll fry the bastard, I'll fucking shred him…

Alex felt like cheering. Walsh deserved everything Alice was imagining and more. She took a seat beside the mayor, trying not to let her thoughts show.

"Have a seat," Tomas said sarcastically. "What's this about the pictures on the victim?"

"Not pictures, Tom, runes. I've come across them before. I was asked to help on a case in L.A. where the victims were killed and left with these little clay tablets beside them."

Tomas nodded. "The runes?"

"Right. I spent a lot of time studying them. I was trying to make them spell out something that would identify the killer. As it turned out, it didn't work, but I did learn something that might help you out on this case. The FBI was called in and I got to know one of them—Special Agent Freemont. He showed me an old case file that he thought might help me figure out what the runes meant. They're a close match for those carved into Sharon."

Tomas' eyes narrowed. "How close?"

Alex hesitated and went out on a limb. "Very close. Almost exact."

Tomas picked up his phone and began dialling. "Freemont you said?"

She nodded.

"Can you remember the case number?"

"No, but I'm sure he will if you—"

Tomas raised his hand. "Hello? Yes, I need to contact a Special Agent Freemont. Yes, I'll hold." He glanced at Alex.

"How well do you know this Freemont?"

Alex frowned. "What has that got to do with anything?"

"Just wondering."

"The hell!" she said, her eyes flashing. "He's a friend, a *good* friend."

Tomas' face blanked. "I see."

What did you expect? Of course there have been other men in her life. You knew there would be. Yeah, but a feebie? It's your own fault. You didn't exactly make her want to stay, did you? Oh shit, I hope she can't hear me. Stone, stone, stone!

"I see," he said again.

He didn't see really, or rather, he saw what she had made him see. It served him right for prying. Freemont was an overweight, slightly balding, and very married man in his forties. He had a mind like a steel trap and was frighteningly good at his job. He was a crack shot and had been the one to take down the killer in her rune case. He was one thing more—a very good friend of hers, just as she had said. So she wasn't lying and didn't have to feel guilty.

Alex listened as Tomas introduced himself and then said hello herself when he put Freemont on the speaker.

"How the hell are you, Alex?" Freemont said. "I heard about what happened. Damn fools don't know what they're throwing away by letting you go."

Tomas' eyes narrowed and Alex hastily steered the conversation to safer ground. "I'm fine, John. Listen, I need a favour."

"Shoot."

"Do you remember a case we worked on about two years back?" she asked, hoping he would say he did.

"We worked a few."

She leaned forward intently. "The rune case?"

"Uh huh, I remember it. Big news back then. You did good."

"Not good enough," Alex disagreed. "But do you remember a case file you showed me? I can't remember the file number or the name, but it had a lot of pictures of runes."

"A serial wasn't it?" Freemont said over the sound of his rapid typing at a keyboard.

"I think so."

"Yeah, I got it. File number #0908-2678/fd233. The perp was one Craig W. Smythe. He raped and tortured thirteen women all told—took trophies, the works. Classic profile for a serial. He was one sick puppy."

Alex crossed her fingers. "Can you fax me the file?"

Silence.

"John, are you still there?"

"Listen, Alex, I owe you a few favours, but I could get my butt in serious trouble if the powers that be found out I was showing a civilian our files. Strictly speaking, I shouldn't have shown it to you back then."

Goddamnit, I need that file!

Alex winced at the ferocity of Tomas' thought. The burst of frustrated anger made her want to massage her temples it was so strong.

"Agent Freemont, this is Sheriff Edwards again. Would it help if I made the request official?"

The mayor seemed distracted. Alex concentrated on what she was thinking for a moment.

I don't believe in voodoo. What's really worrying is that I trust Tom, and he does believe in it. Where the hell does that leave me? And what about the election? They'll crucify me if they find out I signed off on using a witch as a civilian consultant. Especially after what Walsh printed in that rag of his. Good Christ, I'm screwed.

Alex raised an eyebrow in amusement. She couldn't resist temptation and whispered, "I'll vote for you."

—!—

She winced. Alice's shock was like a knife jabbed into her

brain. There were no words or decipherable thoughts behind it, just shock, like an intense burst of static.

"Wha… what do you mean?" Alice said, turning to look at her.

"The election. I'll vote for you."

Oh my god!

Alex grinned.

"Hell, yes, of course it would," Freemont was saying. "*Are you making an official request?*"

"I have a seriously dead woman here," Tomas said, leaning toward the speaker. "She has markings cut into her that Alex says will match your Smythe case."

"*No shit?*" Freemont sounded intrigued.

"Nope."

"*Okay. Fax me the forms and I'll get my boss to sign off on it ASAP. I'll get a copy to you first thing in the morning. Good enough?*"

Tomas nodded. "Good enough, and thanks."

"Thanks, John," Alex said, climbing to her feet. She thought it best to leave now while things remained amicable. The mayor was already a gibbering wreck inside. "I'll leave you to discuss it with Tom. It was good to hear your voice again."

"*Same here, Alex. You keep safe now.*"

"I plan to. Bye."

"*Bye.*"

Alex opened the door and left.

* * *

3~The Hunt Begins

Chores could be, well... a chore, but Alex enjoyed looking after her small menagerie and didn't consider it a chore at all. She had grown up on The Yorke Place helping her grandparents run it. Even back then, it hadn't been what one would call a prosperous money making operation. It had declined into a self-sufficient homestead, rather than a business, years before her parents died and Alex moved here. The fields were wild meadows now except the closest one. Her grandparents had used it to grow food enough for their own needs, and although Alex didn't have their expertise, she still grew vegetables there. She kept pigs in a fenced off section of that field, mainly because it was close, but also because the spring ran through one corner of it making it really easy to keep them watered. They loved messing about in the sloppy mud bordering the stream, and if it made them happy, it made her happy. The chickens, well they just had the run of the place but tended to stay near the barn opposite the house; probably because Alex fed them from the porch and couldn't throw their feed much farther than that.

So her chores were pleasures mostly. Living alone with only animals for company, she had found things to like about nearly everything. Not mucking out the horse stalls, she wasn't a complete lunatic yet, but everything else about living alone on a farm she had found ways to enjoy. This was her life, it was the only one she had or would ever have, and by the goddess, she was determined to enjoy it or die trying!

Alex grinned at the whimsical thought.

That morning she had fed the chickens and turned finding their eggs into a treasure hunt. She won. She groomed the horses and turned them out to run and play in their pasture. She sat on the top rail of the fence to watch them for over an hour, listening to their soothing thoughts and using them to wash away last night's nightmare. Although she owned both horses, she considered Nuisance Jenn's horse because Jenn preferred him to Smokey's more even-tempered temperament. Alex would ride them both later; she doubted Jenn would have time to ride until after she caught Sharon Brydon's murderer.

Alex closed her eyes and reached out to the web. It was like stretching an underused muscle and she groaned in pleasure. It felt good to let go. With no people near, she could do that without fear. The web reached back to claim her, almost joyous in its welcome. It was a gentle reunion, not always so and Alex relaxed a little more. The Yorke Place was hers, her home, her place, and it knew her well. The web never hurt her here at the centre of her own power, but it could and was more likely to do so the longer she shut it out. It didn't like that. The web could try to overwhelm her to teach her a lesson like the time at Blake's Ranch. Sometimes the web hurt to touch anyway, regardless of how long she had withdrawn from it. She didn't know why, but it was almost as if people gave it a different awareness, a spiteful personality bent upon chastising her. It really could be true for all she knew. There was none to teach her after all. She had to make it up as she went along. People meant pain one way or the other.

Her chores complete except for mucking out, Alex used the web and reached out to her fence line—the borders of The

Yorke Place—looking for wrongness. Was anything out of place, anything to show the Shadowman was aware of her? No, nothing. Everything was fine. No incursions of foul magic, or strange shadows, or weak places in the web? None, the web whispered back, the cycle of life and death—the balance, the natural order of things—was undisturbed. The goddess forbid, were there any cut threads like Sharon's poor tree? The web seemed to shy away from her awful thought, but then it edged close again. No, it whispered, nothing like that. Everything is as everything should be. The pigs were fed and happily making more pigs as nature said they should around this time of year, and the chickens were doing what chickens always do. The horses were full of the joy of summer. Katy lay curled up on the porch watching everything, and the lazy cat felt all was well.

Alex put a lot of faith in Katy's good sense.

She opened her eyes and pushed the web away, sealing herself off again despite the web's protests. It was never good for her to forget who she was. The web was a temptress, making her want to stay connected all the time. Its power could invigorate but it also consumed. Like a drug, it would addict. Forever trapped, she would never leave The Yorke Place. It was hard enough leaving now when she knew that she would have to deal with people, but at least she could still venture into town if she was careful and went prepared. She would fight to keep what little of her life she had remaining.

"No rest for the wicked," she said and jumped down from her perch and headed for the stalls and the mucking out she had been putting off all morning.

An hour or so later having finished in the stalls and after taking a shower, Alex was eating lunch in her kitchen and thinking about going for a ride when she heard a car pull up outside. She turned toward the window overlooking the yard already reaching out toward her visitor with the Sight. She flinched and pulled back, hastily raising her barriers as high and hard as she could. Tomas had come for a visit.

"Joy," she said with a long-suffering sigh. She pushed herself to her feet muttering under her breath and feeling her plan for a nice afternoon on horseback slipping from her grasp. If he was here, it meant someone was dead. "Damn."

She met him at the door. He stood there with his hat in hand looking smoking hot in his uniform. Goddess he looked good. He was still using the gym regularly, he must be; his biceps strained the short sleeves of his uniform shirt, and his chest looked as solid with muscle as ever. He had gained a little weight around the middle during the years she had been away, but it suited the rest of him. Without that tiny flaw, he would have looked over muscled like a middle-aged man trying to recapture his youth and keep up with the kids. His dark glasses hid his eyes from her, but she knew they were full of hurt and stubborn unfulfilled need. They always were when they looked at her. His eyes blamed her, and accused her, and tortured her with memories of the past. In their depths, she always saw regret but no forgiveness, and that angered her because she had done nothing that required his forgiveness. She was born this way it wasn't her choice. If anything, he should be on his knees begging her forgiveness for shunning her back then! He would never get it, and maybe that's why he never asked for it. He knew deep down he had destroyed something good beyond repair. She didn't need to see his eyes, this close, his life thread hummed in her mind despite her barriers being up and at Defcon One. He could do that to her no matter how tight she shielded against him. If he touched her... well, he better not that was all. She didn't know how to keep him out if he touched her.

One hand reached down to tug his gunbelt higher to settle it on his hips and that broke the spell. "Hi," he said. "Can I come in?"

Alex was holding the line against him like a soldier defending territory. She held the door open, one hand on the door post the other holding the door half shut with her body in the gap barring entrance. She stepped back, silently inviting him inside.

Tomas stepped inside and waited for direction. Alex closed the door and led him to the sitting room rather than her kitchen. He didn't need to see that she had dirty dishes in the sink. She gestured to the couch and claimed the armchair to keep some distance. The table between them provided some safety.

"What's up?" she said already knowing what it had to be. Sharon's killer had struck again. She would bet money on it.

Sitting on the edge of the couch, he leaned forward resting his forearms on his thighs and played with his hat, sliding it between the thumb and fingers of both hands between his knees. His hands slid together and apart rotating the hat, slide turn, slide turn... Alex forced herself to look up and found his eyes. He must have taken the glasses off when she led him in because they were hooked into the top pocket of his shirt now. His eyes were naked, and yes, the familiar accusation and hurt was there as it always was.

"I have some good news, some bad news, and some worse news," Tomas began.

"No games," she snapped.

Tomas frowned. "I... fine. Good news first then. Your cheque is in the post. You're officially my civilian consultant. The mayor signed off on it. You'll get your usual rate."

"How do you even know my usual rate?"

"It's on your website," Tomas said.

"Oh," she said lamely. Of course it was, together with details of her more interesting cases. Well, those she was allowed to talk about anyway. "Okay. I already knew the mayor had agreed. That time in your office. She told me."

"Told you, right," he said with sarcasm heavy in his tone.

"Don't start. If all you came to do is tell me this then you wasted the trip. You could have told me over the phone. If you came to badger me about my methods, you can leave right now."

Tomas sighed. "I came out here to collect you. That's where the bad news and worse news comes in. I have another scene I need you to look at."

Alex nodded. "I guessed it was something like that, and before you scowl at me, I'm not in your head, Tom. I guessed, just *guessed!*"

His face cleared of the impending storm.

"So he killed again. Same MO?"

Tomas nodded. "Pretty much. Some differences, a lot actually but it's him. The victim is a guy this time, that's one difference, he was killed indoors, but the eyes, heart, and runes are all the same. We kept that out of the media. It's not a copycat. It's him."

"Okay I believe you. I told you that night he was practiced at this. I wouldn't be surprised if he has other bodies hidden out there somewhere. Older kills from before he got good at it."

Tomas nodded accepting that.

"So you want me to take a look at the body?"

"Yes but," Tomas sighed. "This is where the worst news comes in. The mayor ordered me to play nice with Radford. I had to let him do his thing." He raised a hand to placate her as her temper flared. "I know you don't like it, Alex, but it's the best I could do. It was part of the deal. I play nice with him, and the mayor let's me use you."

Alex nodded reluctantly. "In your office she was worried about my voodoo," she said and Tomas winced at the acid dripping from her words. "I guess I can understand, but my rules aren't just for fun, Tom. I'll be lucky to get anything worthwhile from a contaminated scene." Her eyes narrowed when he looked glumly at his hat. "Okay, out with it. What more?"

Tomas sighed. "We found the body yesterday. It's in the

morgue now."

Alex shot to her feet. "You have got to be kidding me! No, absolutely not!"

"I couldn't help it, Alex," he pleaded. "You can still walk the scene can't you? Even if our chances are slim, it's worth a try isn't it? And I stalled the coroner. He'll wait on the autopsy until after you're done. That's got to be good enough. I couldn't put Radford off. He wouldn't stand for it again, and would have gone straight to the mayor and probably the Chronicle too. I'm pretty sure he was our leak last time. Can't prove it, but I think it was."

"Get me close to him and I'll confirm it for you," Alex snarled. "Goddess curse it all! You don't know what it's like for me, Tom. Morgues are... they're not good places. For me I mean. Not good for me. I'll see things in there, all the time. I can't turn it off there," he voice dropped to a whisper. "The last time I tried I fainted."

Tomas looked up sharply at that. "In L.A?"

Alex grimaced. She wouldn't tell him that she'd had nightmares every night for weeks afterward. "Yes, but that isn't what Freemont was talking about. Different case; my last for LAPD. They didn't force me out, I left, but they didn't try to stop me."

"Tell me," Tomas said. "Freemont said you weren't to blame."

Alex scowled. "Freemont has a big mouth. It *was* my fault; I don't care what anyone else says. I fucked up and people died. I was sure I knew who the next victim would be in a serial we were working. I'd been having dreams... well you know what I can do. I told the guys, and they believed me because I was always right," she said bitterly. "They put a watch on her hoping to catch the guy, but it turned out I was completely wrong. I wasn't dreaming about the next victim, I was dreaming about the *perp!*"

Tomas winced. "Female serial killers are rare."

"Not that rare. The cops got her in the end, but not until she killed twice more."

"But if they were watching her?"

Alex shook her head. "They were watching her building to protect her, not apprehend her," she said bitterly. "When nothing happened for a few weeks they pulled out and worked the case the old fashioned way. I was still dreaming about her, but the cops stopped listening. Then she killed two college kids and a witness finally gave a good description. The cops recognised her right away from the protection detail they had tried. Those two kids died because of me. No one said it outright, but they were all thinking it. And before you make excuses for me, you know I mean it when I say *I know* they were thinking it, Tom."

Tomas looked away from the pain on her face and nodded. "It's in the past. What about the morgue thing?"

Alex grimaced, might as well bring it all out there in the open. "Ghosts are strange things, not at all what people believe they are."

"Ghosts?" Tomas spluttered. "Don't tell me they're real, because I really would be happier not knowing that."

"You're not the only one, and they're not real if you think real means they're lost souls with something left undone. We aren't talking Ghostbusters and feeling all funky when you get slimed here."

Tomas grinned. "Love that movie."

She knew he did. "Bear in mind that I'm self taught. I haven't found anyone to teach me about this stuff. The best I've figured is that magic or power or whatever you want to call it is everywhere and in everything. People, plants, animals, even rock. When something dies, magic is released. The problems start when that something is a person, their magic sometimes hangs around and it doesn't like being dead."

"Doesn't like it?"

Alex shrugged. "I'm making this up as I go. I'm just

explaining what it feels like to me. I could be completely wrong, but it feels like magic wants to be in things or people. It doesn't like... *not being*," she winced at her poor attempt at describing it. "I think it's attracted to people; especially to people like me who have a lot of it already. Magic wants to be in people if possible, I mean if I'm right it will be attracted to a live person before it will settle for anything else."

"Oh..." Tomas said and his eyes widened as comprehension dawned. "Oh crap."

"Exactly. A morgue is full of dead people with magic leaking out. Over the years it saturates the place."

"So morgues are what, ghost batteries... ghost magnets?"

"Either," she shrugged. "Both. Ghost aren't souls, I don't think they are anyway. I think magic absorbs our memories and personalities through contact while we live, and then it all leaks out of us when we die. Sometimes it hangs about trying to find a new host. Or maybe it doesn't understand its body is dead and starts looking for it. I have no idea, but I do know that morgues are a trap. Once in there, the only way out is inside someone like me; someone with magic enough to free it."

"So they're like a photocopy of us, but *not* us?"

"I guess. Souls... I don't know about souls, but I like to think they're the original and they just move on to what comes next."

"What happens to the ghost if the body isn't found right away?"

Alex shrugged. "Like I said, sometimes it hangs around but mostly it's absorbed by the web—living things nearby like plants and animals. Cities don't have as many sources of green things, and that's why I think magic is weaker there. I can always feel the difference when I go into town."

Tomas nodded. "If you can't go into the morgue I'll understand."

Alex frowned. "I can go in, but it's harder to do anything

once inside because I have to defend myself."

"The ghosts attack you?"

"They want inside me," Alex said and rolled her eyes at Tom's grin. "Get your mind out of the gutter! I'm being serious."

"I am too," he said with a leer.

She ignored him, always safer. "In a morgue I have to keep my defences high to stop all that crap merging with me. I usually lower my defences to work, and it's harder to do anything if I don't. I will see them everywhere; they're not usually a pretty sight. The time I fainted, I was overwhelmed. There were too many to fight. Do you know how many deaths L.A sees per month?"

Tomas shrugged. "A lot."

"There were twenty-five to forty murders per month when I was there depending on all kinds of factors. Even the weather affects it. Then add the deaths due to natural causes. Imagine how many bodies go in and out of those ghost traps we call morgues during the lifetime of the building."

Tomas shuddered.

Weeks of nightmares followed her fainting spell. She suspected the reason was that some of the ghosts had indeed managed to escape the morgue inside her, and that the dreams were real memories merging with her own. It made her feel ill thinking about it. Her magic was strong and had assimilated them until they were just a part of her, but she had to wonder what the result would have been if she hadn't been as strong as she was. Would she have been the one assimilated? Would her body be walking around with a different person at the wheel? She shivered not liking the possibility. For all she knew it wasn't possible and the nightmares were just dreams based upon what she had seen in the morgue, but something deep inside whispered warnings that she would like to heed. She couldn't though, not if she wanted Shadowman caught.

"Let's get this done," Alex said pushing to her feet.

"The scene?"

Alex nodded. "Scene first, and then the morgue."

"You're sure?" Tomas said.

"Don't tempt me to chicken out, because I will and then you're screwed and I'm down a couple of thousand bucks."

Tomas grinned, but he could see the worry on her face. Alex tried to smooth her features and must have succeeded because he nodded and headed for the door.

* * *

4~Morgue

Alex knew death had visited the house as soon as Tomas parked his cruiser in the drive. She did not need to enter to know it was full of memory and death. Knowing the body was missing, she could have searched the house from the comfort of the car and lost nothing by it, but she had to go in and make a good show for Tomas. The city had to get its money's worth after all. People unfamiliar with her work would not understand if she didn't at least walk the scene, so she released her seat belt and climbed out of the cruiser to follow Tomas to the front door.

Deputy Chase was on guard and bright yellow crime scene tape decorated the front yard. All it did was draw attention, and a small number of gawkers were still clustered along the sectioned off area along the sidewalk. Alex wondered why they were still there. Interest usually waned when bodies left the scene in her experience. She surveyed faces while Tomas spoke with Chase and then realised. They were here to see her. That damn Chronicle headline.

"Alex?" Tomas said. He was standing in the open door. "Coming?"

Alex nodded and gave Chase a smile as she passed him. "My fans are gathering."

Tomas frowned at them. "Chase, keep an eye on the crowd. Keep them off the grounds. Call in backup if you need it."

"Yes sir, Sheriff."

Tomas nodded and closed the door. "It's all yours, Alex."

Alex turned to survey the room. From the outside the house looked like any other, a family sized house split into two levels. Bedrooms upstairs and living areas on the ground floor. Probably a basement too, though she couldn't see any access to it yet. She was standing in the main living space and wondered if perhaps the layout had been modified because if this were hers, she would have preferred a lobby or entrance hall. She didn't like walking off the street directly into the living room this way.

Tomas watched silently and out of the way as Alex explored the house. When she left a room he followed without comment, and she appreciated the courtesy. Being scrutinised while working was something she had become inured to. Having to deal with fool questions as well was annoying.

Alex knew immediately that there was a problem with the house but didn't say anything. She explored upstairs first because she knew there wouldn't be anything to find there and wanted to get those rooms out of the way. Four bedrooms, all neat and tidy; no blood as expected and no residuals. No signs of violence. Residuals, a nice safe word she used for magic pretending to be ghosts. If her theory was right, the word fit. Two of the bedrooms had naked beds, no blankets or sheets, obviously unused guest bedrooms. She opened closets and drawers at random knowing they would be empty. They were. The bathroom was clean and the last two bedrooms were neat but in use. Clothes on hangers and in the drawers. She supposed even drug dealers needed storage, and this house was definitely a dealer's home. She had sensed it the moment she entered. She was sure Tomas knew it too, but he was letting her do her thing... or it was another test. It had better not be. She was tired of performing like a trained monkey.

Down the stairs now and heading for the back of the house where the violence was waiting for her. She stepped into the kitchen but stopped on the threshold. Yes, this was the place. Old and new violence layered one upon the other. Tile was easier to clean she imagined. Probably why he chose the kitchen, but it wouldn't have been her first choice. Cooking dinner in here after murdering someone would take a certain kind of ruthlessness she didn't possess. She studied the white cabinets on the walls, noted the exits one of which led to the back yard, the other she assumed into a utility room. Maybe there was a way down to the basement in there. She was sure there was one, and frowned. Why did she think that? She felt it, and that meant there was something interesting down there. The centre island was coated in dry blood. It looked like an altar set up to worship a sick false god. The blood had dried thickly, but must have run like a river when fresh as it had poured over the sides to stain the white cabinet doors and puddle on the floor.

"Okay, he we go," Alex said. "No matter what happens don't touch me. You remember what happened that night at Blake's Ranch? It would be worse here."

Tomas swallowed. "I remember."

"Good."

Alex lowered her defences and stepped into the room reaching out to the web. It slammed into her, and she staggered. Tomas started forward but aborted the movement in time not to grab her. Alex gritted her teeth and wrestled the web into doing her bidding. It was determined to fill her up, but she didn't want that. She wanted it to show her what had happened here. She insisted it show her, willed it, but it was a slippery sucker. It kept slipping around her and trying to get inside. This is what she had tried to tell Tomas before. The web acted different around people and the guy who had lived here was, had been, a right bastard. Alex snarled and pushed the web back intending to raise her shields again, but just then, the web slackened its attack. She didn't trust that, but it seemed sincere when she started to see what she came for. She took a relieved breath and moved further into the room.

She flinched as the ghostly image of a man shot her, but it was the past she was seeing and she wasn't the target. The dead man lying at her feet was. She stepped back. She had been standing in his corpse. She circled the body. It was a young man. He had tattoos on the backs of his hands and a stud in his nose. His hair was dark and he had a three-day stubble from lack of shaving. His eyes were open and staring at her, at nothing rather. He looked half-white half something else. Part Hispanic she guessed. Good looking, she liked his type except for the fact he was a scumbag dealer like his killer.

Alex looked away for a moment and the body disappeared. The killer walked through her, making her shiver, and disappeared.

"Anything yet?" Tomas asked. His composure had reached its limit apparently, and the questions were spilling out. "What did you see there? We found the body on the island."

"That's obvious. Your victim was a murderer and drug dealer. I'm sensing he was middle management, dealing to the street level pushers. I saw him kill one just now. Don't know why but easy to guess."

"Short on his payment probably," Tomas said. "I'll get a sketch artist to work with you after. Might be one of our cold cases."

Alex nodded and went back to work.

She saw the same guy again, this time beating someone to death while two others held the victim's arms. She circled the scene memorising the face as he slowly destroyed it. That one faded replaced by another and another until she gave up. All the faces were blurring together. She could give Tomas only the first two, but this guy was responsible for a dozen or more. Shadowman had done everyone a favour by killing him. It didn't make her feel any better about him though. He was evil, worse than his victim here. She felt it.

"Too many deaths to count," Alex said and Tomas shook his head in wonder. "Bodies never surfaced?"

"No. I mean sure, we get one now and then. Had two murders last year, but this? No."

"Looks like you have a problem then," Alex said. "This many in one place is unusual; he wasn't worried about being caught. Means he had a sure fire way of making corpses disappear or he has protection."

Tomas scowled. "None of my people would cover this up."

Alex shrugged. "Sure, whatever you say."

Tomas scowled harder.

It was time for the main event. Alex approached the island and touched one finger to the blood. Instantly a new reality arose around her, but it wasn't the one she expected. The island was sparkling clean and there were no bodies. Shadowman wasn't even present. What the hell? The dealer came into the room followed by another man. She recognised him, and the realisation excited her. It was the same man; the driver of the car Shadowman used to kidnap Sharon. She watched him talking to the dealer wishing for an audio track, but wishing did no good. She tried to lip read, but it was pointless. She had no skill in that. The dealer disappeared through the door into the utility room and she followed. There was no other exit and she frowned. She had been so sure...

The dealer faded through the wall at the far end and then came back the same way with a bulky backpack. He gave it to the driver and the scene faded away. Alex turned in a circle noting the washing machine and tumble dryer. The shelving at the far wall attracted her attention. The dealer had walked through it. Couldn't have, but her visions didn't lie.

"Tom, there's something odd about this wall. I saw your dead guy walk through here."

Tomas cocked his head considering her words and then

marched up to the shelving. He pulled and pushed against each shelf, but gained nothing, and then crouched down to study the floor. A moment later, he grunted in surprise and ran a hand over the floor. Alex bent to look. There were scratches in the linoleum, and by the shape, she guessed the shelves would swing out like a door. Tomas stood and started hunting for the latch. It didn't take him long to have the secret door open.

Alex peered down the darkened concrete stairway uneasily. She had known there was a basement, but didn't know why she knew. There was something down there that called to her, and that limited whatever it was to a few things, mostly dead things or magic. She swallowed. She didn't want to go down there, but she didn't want to let Tomas down either. Mostly, she didn't want to appear weak. She forced herself to move carefully down the steps and into the basement. Something tickled her cheek and she nearly screamed before she realised it was the pull string to a light fixture. She gasped in relief and switched on the light.

"Tom, I think I found where the bodies went," she called up the stair. He came down to see. "Clever."

"Clever," Tomas agreed staring into the pit. "And disgusting. Fill the pit with acid, drop the body in, and presto; no evidence except for a few gold fillings. I think I saw on the Discovery Channel that gold doesn't dissolve in acid. Noble metals are resistant to it and corrosion. I'll have Radford come back and clean this out. Might be something at the bottom."

Alex grinned. "Fancy you watching educational shows. Will wonders never cease?"

Tomas grinned back. He turned around to check the rest of the basement. "That isn't an air conditioner," he said looking a machine over. He followed the ducting across the ceiling until it attached to a hood over the pit. "Damn, he thought of everything didn't he?"

"What is it?"

"It's an extraction hood, like you use in the kitchen, except this one is an industrial model. Heavy duty filters. Acid gives off some nasty fumes, and then there's the stink of the bodies. I bet the duct and filters are full of nasty stuff. Radford will love it."

"Your dead guy came down here to get a backpack. He gave it to the driver I saw at Sharon's scene," Alex said as she wandered the basement poking into things. She had Tomas' undivided attention now. "If I were to guess, I would say it was full of money. Could be wrong, but I didn't get the sense that Shadowman cared about drugs. Everyone needs money."

Tomas' eyebrows went up, but he was considering the possibilities. Whatever he decided, he shook his head and said, "Doesn't really matter either way. We're looking for someone responsible for multiple murders, not bring down a drug cartel... would be a nice bonus though."

Alex nodded but she didn't agree about Shadowman's goals. If she knew what he wanted the money for, maybe she could use the knowledge to find him. She helped Tomas search the basement but she was starting to believe Shadowman had taken everything with him. It made perfect sense to her. He probably killed the dealer for his product and the cash he kept here. Killed the golden goose. That meant he must be ready to move on.

"There's nothing here," Alex said. "He took it all."

"You saw that?"

"No, it's a guess."

"Don't guess, Alex, please. I can do that. I need certainties."

Alex shrugged. "Fair enough," she said but wondered when Tomas had started to think of her *mumbo jumbo* as a bona fide source of certainties. He had always professed not to believe in her abilities. "We might as well head out. Nothing else to find here."

Tomas nodded but didn't move. He stood with hands on hips scanning the basement as if he expected clues to pop out in a shower of sparks. Alex left him to it and climbed the stair. She didn't hang around in the kitchen for him, just in case something showed up, but instead beat feet to the front door and stepped outside. Big mistake.

Cameras flashed and questions were yelled. "For the love of..." she sighed.

Chase had kept them back, but he hadn't been able to stop them from waiting on the sidewalk for her. His backup was preventing them blocking Tomas' cruiser, so she scampered that way ignoring them and keeping her face turned away from the cameras. Not that it stopped them from yelling inane questions they knew she wouldn't answer, and filming the back of her head. She got in the car. Lucky for her Tomas hadn't locked it, probably relying upon the badge on its side and lights on its roof to deter thieves. She snorted at what she knew the guys in L.A would say. Tomas' cruiser would be up on blocks and stripped in minutes there. The crooks were like piranha. She grinned at the thought, imagining a boiling cloud of bodies with hammers and wrenches surrounding his pristine car and seconds later scattering again to leave a stripped skeleton.

Alex slid down in her seat to minimise her exposure to the cameras and folded her arms to wait.

It took Tomas maybe five minutes to leave the house. When he did, he stopped to talk with Chase before heading for the car. Chase got on his radio, probably calling for CSI to come back and work its mojo in the basement. Tomas got in the car and started the motor. He backed out quickly, and left the chaos behind.

"So," Tomas said. "The morgue."

"Yeah," she said not looking forward to this.

"I was wondering if there is a way to..." he frowned and sounded words silently under his breath obviously unsure how to ask. "...to clean? To siphon? Well shit, I don't know what to call it, but is there a way to get all the crap out of the morgue?"

Alex grinned. "By crap I assume you mean the ghost photocopy thingies?"

He pointed a finger at her with a mock glare. "Is that the technical term?"

"Beats me. I told you before that I'm making this stuff up as I go along."

Tomas nodded. "Is there a way?"

Alex frowned. Actually it was a good question and not as stupid as it sounded. Magic flowed naturally and it could be directed. If ghosts really were made of magic as she thought, then in theory she should be able to make them move. She knew they weren't trapped beyond recovery. Some of them had managed to escape using her body after all. That was something she was determined would not happen again. So again, in theory they could escape but only with help.

"In theory, there should be a way to *siphon*," she nodded at him for thinking up the word, "to siphon them out of the walls or wherever they've got to, but I don't know how to do it and you would need a living host to hold them. Lastly, you would have to kill the host to let them go free somewhere."

Tomas winced. "But you said any living thing has magic in it. So you could put them into—don't laugh—a potted plant. Or into a dog."

"I like dogs!" Alex said in outrage. "I could never kill a dog."

"The plant then."

Channel a ghost into a living plant? Take it out of the morgue and into the woods. Plant the sucker and let nature take its course. Yes, it would work especially if the location was remote from people. The magic would go back to the web when winter came, but how to channel a ghost one at a time into a plant was beyond her. There was no way a single plant could hold more than one ghost's magic. A dog could probably hold a lot more, and she knew a person could hold dozens—she had done that against her will, but there was no way she would be party to that.

"It would work in theory, Tom, but I don't know how to do it or even how to start. If I did something wrong they would have me in an instant. I won't experiment with something this dangerous. I'm sorry."

Tomas waved that away. "I didn't expect it. I was hoping it would be something that would make it easier for you to go into the morgue and do your thing. Forget I said anything."

Alex nodded and enjoyed the rest of the ride in silence.

Tomas parked the car in the morgue's lot and led Alex inside. They had to sign in and wear visitor badges. Tomas clipped his to his shirt pocket so that it hung over the shiny bar tag with his name on. Alex's shirt didn't have pockets, so she clipped her tag sideways between two buttons on her chest.

Alex was at Defcon One again, and putting everything she had into her shields. Nothing had tried to attack, but they were barely inside the building. The body storage areas were in the basement. The labs and freezers were all down there. The upper levels were administration. The real work of the morgue all happened downstairs. Tomas led her to the elevators and pressed the call button. The doors slid open and they entered together. Another quick button press and they rode the elevator down in silence.

Alex felt the movement like a submarine diving beneath the waves. The further they went, the higher the pressure on her shields became. Unlike her imaginary submarine, she wasn't built to withstand the pressure. She was really working at keeping her composure and her defences strong now. She concentrated on her pillar of rock, sinking everything she had into it. Tomas was watching, maybe wondering why her face looked so grim. She didn't explain that she was expending energy just to stand still beside him and not scramble for the elevator controls desperate to stop it going down any further. It was tiring, like lifting weights. If she slipped, not only would she embarrass herself in front of Tomas, she might well become a taxi for a bunch of dead people—again. That was *not* going to happen *ever* again, no matter what she had to do to avoid it.

The elevator only seemed to take forever to descend. Only three levels, how long could it possibly be? Maybe thirty seconds or so probably, but it seemed like hours as she battled the phantom fingers probing and prying at her defences. She shivered at the feeling of ghostly hands touching her, but they couldn't get inside. What she would do when it was time to work she didn't know, but she would find out.

The doors slid open to reveal a tiled corridor. Brightly painted walls and a multitude of fluorescent light fixtures tried to fool her into believing she wasn't thirty or more feet below ground. Riiight, this wasn't a basement full of dead people; it was an apartment building, or it was a commercial building like a cleaning company. The doors off the corridor didn't lead to cadaver storage areas and laboratories... of course they didn't. The phantom fingers kept stroking stroking stroking, looking for a way in and Alex shivered again.

"Alex, are you okay?" Tomas said, one hand preventing the doors from closing and waiting for her to move.

She nodded shakily and stepped out of the elevator. Tomas followed but then took the lead. He knew where they needed to go and she didn't. As she walked, she kept her eyes forward, centred on Tomas' back, but in her peripheral vision she saw them. The residuals were gathering. She called them that to depersonalise them. They were just impressions, just recordings, not people. They were memory and emotion recorded by magic and trapped here. That was all. So what if everyone thought ghosts were unhappy souls, she knew they weren't, knew it beyond doubt. She knew what souls felt like in her head and ghosts were nothing like them. Her power could tell the difference. That was all that really mattered. By not acknowledging them, she hoped they wouldn't try anything, but it was a forlorn hope. They were already trying to breach her defences with phantom fingers made of magic. They didn't need to crowd close to touch her as real people would; they just stared at her, yearning to merge with her, and those phantom fingers pushed and probed and tried to get inside.

Tomas entered a door and Alex hurried through behind him. She closed the door firmly but moments later the residuals simply faded into existence. They seeped into the room from the walls and floor. Some passed through the door as if it weren't there. They were definitely the same ones from the corridor. She recognised faces and clothing. The styles ranged from decades in the past all the way up to modern day. She tried not to stare at them, but two of the residuals drew her attention. Two children—a boy and a girl—holding hands and staring at her. Without trying, she knew they had died together; brother and sister, together in death as in life. The sight made her eyes go hot. They looked about five years old and didn't attack her. They just stared.

Alex spun away, forcing herself to ignore the children as Tomas greeted a man who had risen from behind a desk when they entered. Alex didn't know anyone here in the morgue. She tried to stay away from places like this. If anyone else had asked her to read a corpse in the morgue, she would have said no fucking way, literally, and then run for her life. Only Tomas could get her here. Only he had a hold on her emotions enough to make her risk it.

Damn him.

"Alex, this is Doctor Hykeham," Tomas said.

Alex braced herself and shook the man's hand. Nothing happened. Her defences were as strong as she could possibly make them, and it kept everything out. Even touching didn't breach them. Yay! Hykeham's hand was dry and his shake tentative. He smiled politely, but he glanced at Tomas for reassurance, and Alex sighed inside; another one who reads the Chronicle and didn't like associating with the *evil witch*.

"Nice to meet you, Doctor Hykeham," Alex said and released his hand. She tried not to wince when he wiped his palm on his thigh as if trying to rid himself of something nasty. "Been waiting long?"

Hykeham stepped away and turned toward the back part of the room. "Not too long, but if you can be done with your... if you can be done quickly, I need to get started on the autopsy."

Alex's eyes were already locked upon the corpse lying on the autopsy table. The hole in his chest, the runes carved in his belly and thighs were obvious. The body had been cleaned of the blood that must have drenched it, probably to make the runes and injuries clearer for the camera. Hykeham had probably thought it couldn't hurt anything to get the preliminaries out of the way. It did. She couldn't explain it so that he would understand, but washing the body, fooling around with it in any way, even undressing it to wash and film it—all of it made her job harder. She would pick up impressions from every person who had handled the body, and would need to discard them without losing any evidence of the killer. If she was very unlucky, she would get nothing about the actual murder, but more than likely, she would get a confused mix from every person involved. That would be a lot of people by now. The cops, the EMTs, and the CSI people at the house, and then the morgue people—Hykeham himself, and anyone who had helped him. Surely, he didn't transport the body, undress, and wash it himself. There could have been a dozen people involved by now.

"Same as before, Tom, no touching no matter what happens," Alex said and looked at Hykeham. "You might not want to watch this."

"Don't worry about me. This is all very fascinating, and besides, I can't leave you alone with the body. Continuity of evidence. You understand."

She did and nodded.

Alex dismissed both men from her thoughts and took a steadying breath. The residuals were still watching her, their eyes boring into her, and those phantom fingers a constant irritant. This was going to be tricky; more than tricky. She already knew her shields prevented anything reaching her, and that was good. They were doing their job. Nevertheless, she needed to touch the body and get to work. She didn't dare lower her defences, but perhaps she could include the body within them? She had never tried to extend shields beyond herself before, but the more she thought about it the more she liked the idea. If she could include the autopsy table within a circle of protection, she could lower her shields entirely and be safe, but with witnesses present, she didn't want to try raising a proper circle. She didn't need more accusations of witchcraft, and besides, she didn't have any of her stuff with her—her athame, the bowls she like to use, even salt. All of it was at home. The circle was out, but maybe she could push her defences beyond her body and hold the residuals out while she worked. She would try, that's all she could do.

Alex stepped up to the table and studied the dead man's face. He had been dead long enough for his skin to turn a little greyish. His sunken eye sockets told her without needing to investigate further that his eyes were gone. Just like the Brydon girl's eyes, they had been sacrificed to Shadowman's ritual. The runes were very clear without blood to obscure them, and Alex took the time to make sure there were no new ones or other differences. There weren't. They matched perfectly, and she was absolutely sure they were cut with the same knife and by the same man. The precision was frightening. Every stroke of the knife, every line was exacting.

Alex turned her attention to the gaping hole in the chest. She leaned forward and swallowed bile as she remembered what Sharon had gone through and what she had been dealing with at night in her dreams. Here it was again. Would she dream about that kitchen tonight, would she be the one held down on that blood-drenched island having her heart cut out? Goddess, she hoped not, but she more than suspected she would be. It was almost standard procedure for her now, reliving what she saw when she did things for the police like this. She was used to it. Used to it, but never resigned. Stupid, but there it was. She always hoped that the next body wouldn't affect her the same way, but it always did.

"Here we go," Alex said and pushed her power out.

Her shields thinned. Alex immediately panicked and let them snap back. She swayed at the backlash, and leaned against the table. That had been less than good. Her hands were shaking and she felt a trickle of sweat run down her temple. This was fucking impossible! Tomas had no right doing this to her. He knew her rules; he knew they weren't frivolous things. There were reasons for everything she did. She had learned what worked and what didn't through trial and error, where every error had led to torment and pain. Damn him for doing this to her. Making her work in the morgue was... it was unforgivable! Coming here was stupid and beyond careless, she had known it was a lost cause when he'd asked her to do it.

But wait, she had gained something from the near disaster. A new lesson learned. Her shields *had* expanded as she'd wanted them too, but doing it had thinned and weakened them. Could she expand them again, but bolster them at the same time? She would have to if this entire visit wasn't going to be a bust. She set herself and tried again.

This time she pushed more power, more magic into the shield as it grew. She did it slowly, not confident of her new ability, but it *was* working. A minute passed, and then two, but eventually it was done. She stood inside something as good as a circle of protection, it held the residuals out anyway, but without a ritual, it did not stand on its own. The table was entirely inside with her, and that was good, but she couldn't just let go of it as she would do with a proper circle. If she did, it would snap back to her like before. Still, it had worked. If she could do her thing inside it, she should be safe.

Alex licked her lips and turned her attention away from the residuals and back to the body. She reached out and touched one finger to the body. She chose the back of one hand to touch, less personal, and stiffened as his essence flowed into her.

His name was Evan Currie and he was an entrepreneur. He always got a kick out of that word. Entrepreneur. He was a self-made man. He had started out in college as the lowest man on the totem pole pushing drugs to the freshmen on campus. It had worked out pretty well, but he knew even then that he wanted more. He had really lucked out when a few of the college girls wanted more and harder stuff, but couldn't pay. He took a risk by paying for the black whack himself and let them have a few freebies. It was good stuff, pure, and after the first few hits, they were hooked. He called in their markers, and the rest as they say is history. It was so damn easy. He had them blowing the college boys and pulling tricks to feed their habit in no time. That's when the money really started rolling in. He was an entrepreneur...

Alex swallowed sickly as images swirled though her head of crying women with haunted eyes. Evan had destroyed so many lives. He deserved worse than he had gotten. He had pimped out girls, taking their money and investing it into drugs. In just a few years, he had climbed high enough that the big boys took notice.

Evan paced. Where the hell were they? They were into him for a lot of money and if they didn't make good on the debt, he would need to run. The boss would skin him; literally flay him alive when he found out where the money had gone. Nothing but a solid profit would save him now, and he hadn't seen a goddamned dime yet!

Damn them, how had they convinced him this deal was a

good idea? How!? The freak had done something to him, he must have. He would never have agreed to this insanity otherwise. He should have killed Russell for introducing them, but John had been so excited by what the freak had shown him, by what he could do, that Evan had to see for himself. Who the hell believed in magic? Certainly not he, but John Russell was a believer. Heaven help him, Evan was too after the freak demonstrated what could be done by sacrificing a bum in his kitchen.

Alex gritted her teeth as she lost the images of Evan in his house and saw Doctor Hykeham preparing the body. She growled under her breath trying to sort through the mess of images and feelings flooding her thoughts. She saw the murder scene again, but through the eyes of the police. It wasn't Tomas. More and more images and impressions pushed into her head, but finally she filtered them out and was solidly back with Evan Currie.

Evan peered out into the night and sighed in relief as John's familiar silver Volvo pulled up outside. Finally. He opened the front door and waited for John to come up to the house, but when the front and rear passenger doors also opened and the freak stepped out with muscle for protection, Evan's relief faded to alarm. John was supposed to come alone.

Alex frowned. The freak was Shadowman, and no matter what she did, she could not resolve his face. John Russell was the driver, and she knew him from the other murder scene. She didn't recognise the last man, the one who rode in the back of the car, but Evan had dismissed him as muscle. She was willing to do the same. The car was a clue, a real live clue, but Tomas would need more than the make, and colour. She touched the body again and tried to narrow her focus to that car arriving.

Evan peered out into the night and sighed in relief as John's familiar silver Volvo pulled up outside.

Alex frowned harder and concentrated, narrowing her view to the license plate. Evan had seen it only briefly, but he had seen it and that was all she needed.

...the night and sighed in relief as John's familiar silver Volvo pulled up outside.

Dammit! More detail, she needed more detail! She forced herself to watch it again, and again, and again.

... John's familiar silver Volvo pulled up outside... John's familiar silver Volvo pulled up outside... John's familiar silver Volvo... silver Volvo... Volvo... Volvo... pulled up... silver... silver Volvo pulled... up... Volvo pulled up... silver... Volvo pulled up outside... up outside... pulled up... Volvo... Volvo... VOLVO!

Alex gasped, and reeled away from the table staggering and clutching her head. She had the number and tried to speak as she went to her knees still clutching her head as the scene replayed in her head over and over. *The pain!*

"What was that?" Tomas said eagerly leaning forward. He had his notebook out and ready. "Say again!"

"License plate..." Alex gasped. "Silver Volvo... same car used to abduct Sharon." Tears of pain ran over her cheeks as the worst headache in the world thundered in her head, but she managed to repeat the license plate twice more before she let it all go and frantically tried to shut it out.

She couldn't let go of her sheild, but she did let it slip back to a normal size so that the body on the table was sealed outside. The moment she released her grip on it, it snapped back so violently that her legs went out from under her as if she'd been punched. She desperately reached for it before all her defences went down, and hastily centred her thoughts on the pillar of rock. The residuals howled as they missed their chance to get in, and raged around the room. Her eyes followed them fearfully as they smashed into her shields over and over. They were very agitated now, and she wanted out of here.

Tomas wanted to help her up but he didn't dare. The doctor looked spooked, but he moved forward to help and would have touched her, but Tomas was there and stopped him. Alex pushed herself up like a drunk, and staggered toward the door.

"Have to get out... have to... can't..." she stammered breathlessly. "Got to get out of here."

"Alex?"

She shook her head and tried to run for the elevator, but her knees were like rubber and she barely made them move into a staggering walk. Behind her, she heard Tomas thank Hykeham and then hurry out to catch up. She slammed her palm repeatedly on the call button whimpering when the doors didn't open. The residuals were trying to get in again. She spun and slammed her back against the closed doors pushing back as if she might slip through the crack between them. She stared at the residuals as they milled back and forth, and flinched as some of them darted toward her, but she felt no impact. Suddenly Alex fell backward as the elevator doors opened. She forced herself into the corner and hit the controls. The doors slid shut and the elevator started its climb. Alex whimpered at the pain and the feel of the residuals trying to hold on to her, but the pressure was easing as more and more lost their grip on her shields and fell away howling back into the depths. The submarine was heading for the surface again. Tomas was talking, but she couldn't understand him and didn't try. All that mattered was that she get outside and into the sun. The doors slid open and she gasped in relief.

Alex staggered toward the glass doors leading to the street, and ignored everything but the sunlit world beyond the doors.

"Miss! You have to sign out. Miss? Your badge, you can't take..."

Alex whimpered and grasped the visitor badge. She ripped

it off and dropped it on the floor before bursting outside. It was as if she had been drowning and now had reached the surface. She sucked in air and trembled. The headache was better, but not gone. Something touched the back of her neck and she spun. Nothing there. Just sensory memories maybe. Something tickled her neck again and she spun again. This time she caught a glimpse of something that drained all the colour from her face. She felt it go as her breathing slowed. Cold sweat beaded on her face. She was going into shock. The ghost children stood before her and smiled as they faded away to join the web.

Alex crumpled to the ground in a dead faint.

* * *

5~Stranger

Alex paced the room like a caged animal, trying to persuade her tired brain that it was all right to sleep, but it wasn't all right. Something was wrong, something was out there. She just knew. She was sick of knowing things she shouldn't. She was sick of always being afraid. She should go out into the dark and drive over there. That's what she should do. He wouldn't know, he wouldn't see her if she were careful. If only she could tell Jenn what she had seen this time, it might make a difference.

Jenn had phoned earlier to tell her that Tomas was following a lead that might see the end to all their worrying. She couldn't be specific, but it seemed someone had seen the car used to kidnap Sharon. Jenn thought the driver might be the actual killer, but she was open to the possibility that he might simply be an accomplice. They were moving on him now and would have him in custody tonight.

Alex knew the driver wasn't the killer, but there was nothing she could point to as proof. He might know where the killer was, but it wasn't him. She could still sense the shadow. The killer, Shadowman, was somewhere to the south of town, she was certain of it.

Night after night, her sleep had been plagued with dreams of Sharon and the runes that meant something important. She couldn't look at the most ordinary things anymore without seeing the shapes of runes hidden among them. She had borrowed books from the library on the subject of Germanic runes in an effort to understand what her dreams were trying to tell her. She now knew what the killer had been saying as he murdered Sharon. It was the names of the runes, incanted like a spell or a prayer. Such incantations had a name, runagaldrar, and were still used until quite recently in Scandinavia.

Alex spun on her heel and began another circuit of the room. It was almost three o'clock in the morning and she desperately needed sleep, but the thought of closing her eyes brought her dreams surging into the forefront of her thoughts. He was out there right now. If she closed her eyes, she could feel the hard seams of the leather gloves he wore, hear his breathing as he ran, smell his rank breath, and then there was the fear. He was afraid. It thrilled her even as the fear clogged her own throat. Was he running from the police? Were they going to catch him after all?

She reached out to him…

Alex gasped and her eyes snapped open when she realised what she was doing. She had been trying to reach him! Oh Goddess, oh Lady what was she going to do? She could feel him out there, and she wasn't dreaming. She was wide awake and shivering, not with cold, but with fear. It was getting worse, or she was getting stronger; it didn't matter which. Shadowman wasn't running from someone, he was running *toward* someone. Someone he feared, someone who was going to die.

Alex used to believe that everyone was basically kind and decent. If you gave them a chance, they would shine. But that was before evil came to town. He was evil; true, burn in hellfire for eternity, evil. She hadn't recognised it in time. Why hadn't she recognised it? Surely she should have. Surely she had this power… this *thing* for just this reason? Why hadn't she sensed his coming before he killed Sharon? She knew why. She had been afraid to open herself to the web. If she had used it, just to look, just to be sure of safety, would she have sensed him approaching? She groaned. She knew she would have. She could feel his evil; of course she would have felt him approaching. It was her fault. All of it. Sharon wouldn't be dead if not for her.

Oh Lady she was scared. She was scared of him and what he would do tonight and other nights until caught, but she was almost more scared of herself and this thing that had taken over her life. She couldn't stop from doing it anymore. She wasn't in control of it, whatever it was.

She had to do something; that was all. She had to do something other than pace all night. She snatched up her keys from the table and stormed out the door, determination etched upon her face. She would drive over there and tell Jenn everything.

Alex slid behind the wheel of her truck and gunned the engine, spewing stones from the rear wheels. She had to be fast. Tom would be there waiting with Jenn and the others, anticipating a phone call from his colleagues in Westwood. She knew what he would say when he saw her, but she couldn't keep this quiet. She would get in, see Jenn, and get out before anyone noticed she was there. That's what she would do.

The beat up Chevy poured oil smoke into the air. It was a wreck, but it was her wreck, free and clear of the finance company. Its dented and rust spotted exterior suited her somehow. She had no need of a fancy vehicle; it wasn't as if she had ever planned on working the farm. It hadn't been worked for more than twenty years. Her grandfather had been the last Yorke to actually make a living from farming and it hadn't been a good living even then. She had inherited the place from him.

Alex's eyes prickled as she remembered him, but she

didn't cry. The hurt was an old one, and time had blunted it. The quick stab of pain was replaced by warmth when she remembered how her grandparents had taken care of her after the fire. She didn't remember much about it—it had happened when she was only six, but she did remember her first days on the farm. They were the best and brightest memories she had.

She downshifted with a crunch of gears, stabbed the brake pedal briefly, and accelerated through the corner just as Jenn had taught her. The old truck hugged the curb as well as the police cruiser Jenn had used to teach her. *Well almost*, she thought as she imagined the scolding her friend would give her for using her lessons to break the law.

The road ahead was empty. The trees and bushes blurred past, only briefly illuminated by her headlights. She knew the road like the back of her hand and drove fast. She was well over the speed limit, barely under her truck's top speed, when she noticed the headlights in her mirrors. She automatically took her foot off the gas, but she didn't use her brakes. Jenn said it was always a dead giveaway when someone did that. It made cops suspicious when someone braked at the sight of a police cruiser. The officer would assume, rightly in this instance, she was doing something she shouldn't be doing. She allowed the truck to slow and continued for a few miles just under the speed limit. She watched the lights in her mirrors, expecting them to swing wide and overtake her, but they just sat there, uncomfortably close. She let the truck slow a little more. The headlights closed up on her bumper a little and then dropped back to a safe distance again.

And still the car didn't overtake.

Alex licked dry lips and her palms began to sweat. She was a fool to come out alone at night, especially knowing what she did. It could be him, but wouldn't she know? No, she wouldn't. She couldn't drive and use the web at the same time. It took concentration to seek someone in that way. And then there was the fear; she just didn't *want* to do it. She was a fool. No one knew she was out here and the road continued for miles. She floored the accelerator and the truck surged ahead.

The headlights dwindled in her mirrors. She lost them to the night when she crested the hill and sped down the other side. All her mirrors were empty and she laughed shakily. It had been nothing; just another traveller on the road. Nothing to—

"Shit!" she screamed as her headlights revealed a man shielding his eyes directly ahead of her.

She hit the brakes and cranked the steering wheel hard to the left. Tyres screamed and the truck slewed sideways. She fought the wheel, fearing the truck would roll, but she regained control just in time to see the figure go down.

"Oh Lady, no. *I hit him!* Oh no, Goddess no," she panted, still hearing the thud of his body striking the rear quarter of her truck.

Alex jumped out and ran back up the road. She couldn't see him. It was dark, but she should have seen him in the moon glow. She sprinted up the hill, knowing she had gone too far. She must have missed him. She tried to reach out to the web, and succeeded after a brief struggle against panic. Nothing. She couldn't find him. What if he were dead? No, dead didn't matter. She would still sense his thread, even if dull and lifeless. Dead threads took a long time to fade completely, just like Sharon's dead tree.

She ran back to her truck and ripped open the glove compartment. Dashing tissues and roadmaps onto the floor, she came up with a flashlight. She retraced her steps, waving the light at the curbs. The verges were liquid shadow, but the flashlight's beam speared the night, making the shadows flee. There! He lay entangled in a bush. He looked dead.

"Oh please... please don't be dead. I'll do anything."

He groaned.

Before Alex knew it, she had fistfuls of his clothes and was pulling him out from the clawing branches. His eyes opened and looked at her in confusion. They were a startling blue and she caught her breath at the sight of them. He groaned again and his face screwed up in pain. She cursed herself for a fool and checked for broken bones. His left leg didn't look right. It was twisted sideways under him and might be broken. He had a purpling bruise on that side of his face and there was blood, but it seemed superficial. She realised he could have internal injuries and wished she had a phone.

"I'm going for help," she said. "I'll be back."

He clutched her hand, not letting her leave. Confusion roared through her at his touch, making her light-headed. She swayed, blinking rapidly, and tried to fight off the strange feeling. She tried to push it away, but the pressure increased and her vision dimmed.

Alex blinked and shook her head to clear it. What had just happened? She remembered the accident, but everything after that was a blur. Something had happened when he touched her, something strange but sort of familiar... What was she doing? She was staring into a stranger's eyes like a fool when he could be dying!

"Let go, I have to get help."

"Noooo," he moaned. "Please Sister, you help me. Hide me. They come for me."

Alex tugged on her hand. "You're hurt. You might die if I move you."

"I will certainly die if you do not, Sister. I beg you, remember the Pact. Hide me from them."

Pact? Sister?

Alex had no idea what he was talking about, and doubted he did either, but she didn't want to leave him like this. Her place was a long way from here and head injuries could be serious; she might not get back in time. He might wander away or be hit by another car, though his leg might stop him from moving very far. She pulled him carefully onto his good leg, cursing herself for a fool all the while. He would probably sue her, or die on the way to the hospital, or… he sagged in her arms, almost toppling them both to the road. She supported him on the left side, struggling to drag him along without banging his leg.

"You have to try," she gasped. "I know you're hurt, but you have to help me with this. You're heavy."

"I'll… I'll try. Is your steed far?" he said weakly, his head weaving from side to side trying to see.

"My…" she shook her head in confusion. "My truck is just there."

"Truck," he said vaguely. "Where am I, and what manner of beast is that? Its eyes blinded me."

Alex grimaced. He was babbling. "Never mind, just get in."

She manhandled him into the passenger seat, trying to ignore his pained grunts and gasps as she buckled the seatbelt. He was barely conscious by the time she restarted the truck. He blinked slowly at his surroundings. Alex bit her lip at his paleness and, as ever, drove fast.

* * *

Pain was Douglas' constant companion. There were techniques for ignoring such things as the trivialities they were, only he couldn't recall how to begin. The noise of the strange beast was distracting, and his rescuer was more so. He wished she would be more trusting and let him rest. Her magic constantly probed his shields as a tongue probes a bad tooth.

Weakness dragged at him and his leg was a blaze of agony. It was undoubtedly broken. He had broken enough bones in his time to know it needed a splint, and he wasn't looking forward to it. The thought of how much it would hurt made him shudder and break out in a cold sweat. If she would only let him alone for a time, he might find the strength to call power. Perhaps enough to dull the pain and begin a healing chant.

"Hold on, just hold on," she said reaching out and patting his shoulder. "I'll get help, just don't die."

She was much concerned with death, this one. He wouldn't die from a little headache, and he had certainly received worse than a broken leg in his time. Douglas remembered being thrown from his horse when he wasn't much older than seven years. His father had put him straight back in the saddle, taking no notice of his protests, even when it became obvious his arm and ribs were broken. He had completed that day's hunting in a haze of pain, but it had been worth it to see the pride in his father's eyes when they finally rode home. The King had congratulated his father on an excellent day's sport and on his son's fortitude.

Douglas tried to take his mind off his pain by watching the witch. She was as strange as her steed. She was not a young maid, neither was she old. Her manner of dress was strange to him, as was her language. If not for his taufr and the spell he had cast, he would be unable to understand her or she him, which was an unhappy surprise. He was adept at many languages and took pride in his skill at learning new ones, yet hers seemed to defy him a purpose. It was most puzzling, as was this *truck*, which he now understood was no beast or steed at all, but was instead a made thing. Certainly no practitioner of the arts he had ever met could make something so strange, and neither would they want to. It was a noisy, smelly, and unholy way to travel. He glanced outside.

Fast too.

Douglas watched the countryside blurring past the marvellously clear glass, and estimated his speed was at least twice that of the fastest steed in the kingdom, and not once had the *truck* stopped to rest. Of course, such a *truck* would be wholly useless if not for that marvellously smooth road, of which there were none even remotely similar in the kingdom.

To his mind, a good warhorse was still a better way to travel. A horse needed no roads such as this, and was more useful. It was companion on the road, ally in a fight, could forage for itself at need, and stand guard at night. He might be entirely wrong, but he would wager that the witch's *truck* could do none of those things.

She glanced at him. "I'm Alexandra Yorke. Call me Alex, everyone does."

"Forgive me, Lady Alex, I should have introduced myself before now, but under the circumstances..." He shrugged and winced at the pain in his shoulder. "I am Douglas, called Red Hand by some, Duke of Skeldon, Lord of the Fen and Bryansk. Not that anyone lives in Bryansk any more, but I like the sound of it, don't you?"

His attempt at humour fell flat. He could tell by her stiff posture that he had made a mistake with her. Either she thought him a vainglorious fool for bragging, or worse, she didn't believe him at all. He wasn't sure which it was, but either one made him wish he had stopped at: *I am Douglas.*

"Douglas will do," he said, smiling weakly.

The silence stretched out.

He watched her through a haze of pain as she guided her *truck* through the night. The wheel in her hands and the stalks under her feet made it go. He wondered if he might try it sometime. Waves of pain drove thoughts of her strange steed out of his head. He was in danger of passing out. He laid his head back and closed his eyes, trying to concentrate his will. If he could only call power enough to numb the pain...

Everything went black.

The lack of motion woke him. He still sat in the *truck*, but there was no sign of his rescuer. He fumbled for the catch that held the belt across his chest, but before he could release it, Alex arrived and opened the door. She wasn't alone. A man dressed all in pale blue leaned in and stared carefully into his eyes. He said something Douglas did not understand. The man, a mage or healer he assumed, gently parted his hair to find the source of the blood caking his face.

"Is he going to be all right, Doc?" Alex asked. "It was a long way to fall."

Douglas blinked. A fall?

"Hedar dis linsha, eh? Don worreh, Alex," the mage said and then released the belt holding Douglas in his seat.

Alex stepped forward to help, and together they eased him out of the *truck* and into a chair on wheels. Waves of pain drove Douglas toward oblivion, but he fought the darkness back. He dare not be caught unawares; he must stay awake if he was to have any say in matters.

The mage led the way into a large building from which dozens of lights shone through glass windows. The hospice, for that was surely what it was, must have a noble benefactor. So much glass would have cost a formidable amount, as would the amount of lamp oil needed to light such a place.

Alex pushed the wheeled chair up the slope and into the building. As she walked, she leaned forward to whisper. "I told Doc Williams that you fell from the hayloft in my barn. He's a friend of mine, but road accidents are supposed to be reported. You said there was someone after you, so I thought it better to say you were working for me when you fell."

"I thank you, Lady," Douglas said, relieved that his spell was holding her to the correct course. "It would be best if no one knew I am here."

"Just close your eyes and let Doc fix you up. He says your leg is broken, but the cut on your head isn't serious. I'll take care of you, I promise."

Douglas relaxed and closed his eyes, but he didn't let himself sleep. Witches back home could be relied upon to keep their word, but here? He did not know. He didn't even know how far from home he was. He was beginning to fear it was very far indeed—across the eastern sea even.

Alex stayed with him through all the strangeness. A woman washed his face and hands with something that smelled incredibly bad. It stung his cuts and scrapes like fury. There were rooms behind doors with strange writing on them, and something Alex called an *x-ray machine*. It was a magic he had never seen or heard of, one that could see inside his leg to the broken bone.

Next there came an *injection*, and with it all sensation in his leg fled. What a marvellous thing the *injection* was. He sighed in relief. He was finally able to concentrate enough to work another quick spell. This time he directed it at Williams.

"Gis dar khrds jopher?" Williams was saying as the spell took hold. He blinked rapidly and swayed as if about to fall. He stepped back to regain his balance, and cocked his head, as if listening to something only he could hear. "Is..." he shook his head in confusion. "Gis dar khrds gone now?"

Douglas shook his head. "I'm sorry, I was miles away. What did you say?"

"I was asking if the pain is gone now."

"It's quite gone, thank you."

Williams nodded in satisfaction. "Good, good. We can set your leg then."

Douglas tensed, but the marvellous *injection* was still working. His leg might as well have not been there for all the sensation it had. Not only did it not hurt when Williams helped him remove his pants, he felt nothing as Williams straightened the crooked limb and began applying bandaging.

Douglas watched in admiration as Williams plied his craft. He wrapped the leg in a thick layer of cotton bandaging, and then applied something that looked uncannily like the mortar a mason might use. It dried rock hard and held his leg immobile. By the time the cast had set hard, Douglas' eyelids had grown heavy. He blinked and shook his head. He could barely stay awake.

"... keep him in for the night if you like, Alex. It's no

problem."

"Thanks, Doc, but he got hurt helping me. It wouldn't be right leaving him here. If you could help me get him into the truck?"

"No problem."

The cool night air revived him somewhat, and he was able to get back into the *truck* with only a little assistance from Williams.

"Remember to keep the cast as dry as you can. I'll replace it with a fibreglass one once the swelling goes down. That should be in roughly a week's time. Let's say this coming Friday."

Alex slammed the door. "Friday. I'll remember."

Williams nodded. "Put him to bed and let him rest. That's what he really needs." He handed her a small bottle. "Don't forget, no more than four of these in twenty four hours."

"Got it. Thanks for everything, Doc."

Alex climbed into the truck and Williams went back into the hospital. "He knows something's up."

Douglas silently agreed. "But he's your friend."

"Hmmm. He won't say anything, but he'll be thinking all kinds of things about us."

Douglas grinned. "Perhaps in a few days you can tell him of your adventure on the road."

Alex snorted and did something to the *truck* to make it roar. A moment later, they were back on the road. Douglas lay his head back against the seat and tried to rest. Williams was right about that, he did need rest, but not for the reasons Williams thought. When Wallace came for him, he needed to be ready, for he would be fighting for his life.

The *truck's* movement jostled Douglas awake. He blearily glanced outside and then at Alex. "Where do you take me, Sister?"

"My home. It's not far now. Do you know the Yorke Place?"

He shook his head in confusion. "Yorke Place?"

"That's what everyone calls it," Alex said and did something to slow down.

Douglas winced as she pulled on a lever sticking up from the floor. The *truck* made a horrendous noise before turning through a gate. It was a farm they approached. He stared, hardly able to believe it. He had expected a House of the Mother, not this.

"You live here with your sisters?" Douglas asked.

Alex shook her head a little. "I live alone. I have no family left alive."

He frowned; this place was becoming stranger by the moment. No Daughter of the Mother was ever alone, yet he saw no reason for her to lie. The farm was her home and hers alone. Where were her sisters? No family she said… No sisters? No, that wasn't… *couldn't* be right.

"Where in the world am I?" he asked, feeling more and more out of sorts. "I don't recognise your clothes, this *truck*, the road. Not even Guild artificers could make such things. Where am I?"

Alex stopped her truck and turned toward him. "Listen Douglas, if that's really your name, just calm down. This is my home; I own the house, the stables, and the land all around here. You'll be all right. Doc said there was a chance you might have a mild concussion. You're just confused. Let's go inside and get you into bed. You'll feel better in the morning."

Alex opened her door and Douglas mimicked her by pulling the shiny handle on his side. The door creaked open and he fumbled at the belt holding him in his seat. The catch clicked and the belt slid through his fingers. Alex came around to his side and helped him out of the *truck*. He barely held in a scream when he tried to stand. He groaned and almost fell limply into her arms.

"Lean on me," Alex gasped, barely preventing his collapse. "It's not far."

It was all Douglas could do to stay conscious. Waves of agony swept over him, making him swoon. The *injection* must have worn off on the journey. He felt sure he would fall and disgrace himself in Alex's eyes. He was determined not to pass out in her arms. Dignity was the thing.

Show her some dignity, Douglas.

He froze.

"Come on, just a little more," Alex said, trying to urge him up the steps to her home.

Douglas stared over the roof of the house and the blood drained from his face. With a shaking hand, he pointed at the sky. "What... what is that?"

"It's just the moon, silly."

"*No...*" He stared in horror. The moon, she said as if it was the only one and perfectly normal. "By the blessed goddess, I'm lost to the world. Am I dead?"

"You're not dead, and you won't die. Now *come* on!"

Alex dragged him up the stairs and into her home. There was a strange creature standing guard in the middle of the room. It laid its ears back and snarled at him, but the sound it made was more like the hiss of a snake. It was small and black with a white patch on its chest. Needle sharp teeth filled its mouth. He had never seen anything like it. Although small, it was obviously vicious.

"Shoo, Katy!" Alex glanced at him guiltily. "She doesn't like strangers."

"Oh," he said uncertainly as Katy streaked toward him and out through a small hatch in the door. "What is she?"

Alex looked at him strangely. "She's just a cat."

That was a cat? It was nothing like the cats he had seen, and so tiny! Who had ever heard of keeping a cat in the house? Cats back home would sooner eat you than live with you.

Alex led him into another room. It was her bedchamber, or maybe a guest chamber. She did something and light flooded from a lamp hanging overhead. He shielded his eyes and allowed himself to be led to the bed. It was a bed like any other, though brass railings instead of wood seemed extravagant for a farm. It was a relief to understand something. After seeing so many strange things, his brain was swimming in unanswered questions.

Alex crossed the room and pulled drapes across the single window, shutting out the night, and then stepped through another door. She reappeared with a glass of water and offered him one of the *painkillers* Williams had supplied. Douglas obediently swallowed it and chased it with a sip of water.

"Thank you for your care, Lady Alex."

Alex snorted. "It's my fault you were hurt."

"Not so. The leg, yes that was the *truck,* and my ribs and shoulder too, but this," he raised a hand to his bandaged head. "I was attacked before I came here. You're not to blame for any of this. I was stunned and wandered the woods until finding the road. My condition is entirely due to Wallace and his band of traitors."

"Wallace?" she asked, cocking her head a little.

"My attacker."

"You know who did it? I should call the sheriff then."

Douglas frowned, another unfamiliar word. "Who is this sheriff you speak of? Is he the local authority, the lord here?"

Alex snorted. "Tom would love to be treated like a lord. He already acts like one. Lord Sheriff Edwards indeed; he would love that!"

Douglas shook his head as Alex left the room chuckling about Lord Sheriff Edwards.

* * *

Alex left Douglas sitting on the bed and made her way into the kitchen to make some fresh coffee. She could use some, and she felt certain Douglas could too. The phone chose that moment to ring and she snatched it up. "Hello?"

"Alex?"

"Jenn?"

"Yeah, it's me. We just got the word. It's not good news."

"You didn't get him," Alex said numbly.

"Oh, we got him all right, but he's dead," Jenn said in disgust. "It seems your killer figured out we were onto his friend and killed him before we could talk to him."

"Some friend!" Alex snorted.

"Yeah well, anyway, he's dead, but that means we have nothing to link him to Sharon's killer. He's still out there and..."

Alex reached for a stool and sat. "And what?"

Jenn sighed. "And he might come after you. Everyone knows you helped us out, Alex. Tom wants to put you in protective custody."

"No way! You want to put me in jail?"

"It won't be like that. You can stay at my place; we'll surround you with our guys. He won't get near you."

"No," Alex said firmly. She couldn't be near people that way, her... *condition* forced her to live alone, and besides, she wouldn't allow Tom to lock her up like some criminal.

"Be reasonable, Alex. You live alone and miles from town. You're vulnerable out there."

Alex cursed under her breath. "I should have stayed home that night. None of this would be happening if I'd kept my nose out of it."

"You wouldn't have done that," Jenn said, attempting to cajole her friend.

Alex sighed. "No, I guess not."

"I'll pick you up in an hour."

Alex counted silently under her breath and pushed the sudden flare of anger back down. "I'm not leaving my home, Jenn. I don't care what you say or who you send, I'm staying."

"But—"

"You can't take me in without my consent!" she snapped,

starting to lose it and feeling her face reddening. "Tell Tom I'll sue him if he tries. I haven't done anything wrong. Tell him I'll not be locked up for doing the right thing."

There was a brief silence and then, "Alex, it's Tom."

"I'll tell you what I told Jenn."

"No need, I know what you said."

Alex's eyes blazed in sudden understanding. Jenn was his stalking horse; he must have known what she would say to him if he had tried this. "Have you got me on your damn speaker? How many are listening right now you... you... *you prick!*"

"Calm down, Alex. There's only me and Jenn in here. I'll have a car do a drive by your place every hour or two, but you know that won't be enough if he decides to come after you. Be reasonable and let me protect you. Let me bring you in."

"No," she said firmly.

Tomas sighed. "Is there anything more you can tell me, anything at all that might help us catch this guy quicker?"

She hesitated. "Not really, but..."

"But?"

"I think he's still hanging around. Not in town, but south of it."

"How do you know?"

"*I just do!*" she snapped, but then she relented a little. "I can't explain how I know. I tried to tell you once before, remember? Just trust me that I know things, things I shouldn't know but do anyway."

"Okay, okay. I'm going to have a hell of a time trying to get a warrant based on nothing but intuition and mumbo jumbo. Why south of town?"

Alex grimaced in frustration. "I don't know, but I've had this feeling for a couple of days now. There's a shadow over the town, but it's coming from the south."

"A shadow," Tomas said, sotto voiced.

He was just humouring her now. She closed her eyes and counted to ten. She didn't want to be angry; it would make it even harder to persuade him, but Lady it was hard to be civil. "I know how it sounds, but the shadow is him. I know it's him."

"Could you point to it on a map?"

"I have no idea."

"Will you try?"

"I guess so." Alex didn't know if such a thing could work. The shadow was just a feeling of menace. How could she point out a location without going there first? "Tell someone to bring one and I'll try."

"Couldn't you—"

"I'm not coming in!" she snarled.

"I didn't mean—"

"The hell you didn't! If I come down there, you'll persuade me to stay the night, and then it will be two nights. Before I know it, I'll have a permanent room in the jail."

"All right, all right! You can't blame me for trying, Alex. I'll bring your damn map in the morning."

"Fine," she snapped and slammed the phone down.

* * *

6~Lord of the Fen

Douglas' face looked grey with exhaustion when Alex returned with his coffee. Leaving the light off, she sat on the edge of his bed and placed the cup on the bedside table within his reach. He glanced at it and nodded his thanks, but he made no move to drink it. The startling blue of his eyes still had the power to stop her breath, but his face had already become familiar; his tussled hair, his shadowed cheeks and strong jaw. She felt as if she had known him for a long time, but that was silly.

He was different; for one thing, she couldn't hear his thoughts at all, and that was very rare. She couldn't remember the last time she had met someone she couldn't read. She daringly reached out to sweep his hair off his brow and laid a hand there. She felt nothing but hot skin. No images in her head, no voices, just Douglas.

"You're still hot."

Douglas smiled tiredly. "Williams said the injection will deal with it. He seemed a learned man."

Alex nodded. "He is. Your leg is the worst; it will take time to mend, but the rest will be healed in a few days."

Douglas took her hand. "I told you I will be fine; falling from my horse hurt worse. Alex, I must apologise for putting you in this position."

She waved that away. "It was my fault."

"Please, Sister, listen before forgiving me. There are circumstances that you are unaware of. I fear I am ill equipped to explain and you will believe me crazed, but I must try." He took a deep breath. "I am not of your world."

Alex blinked, trying to keep her worry off her face. "Is that all? Well, don't you worry."

"You don't believe me, I understand that. I would not believe were I you, but it is imperative you understand the danger of my being here. When I first realised you were a witch—"

Alex stiffened but Douglas didn't seem to notice. He babbled on about a place called Inari—apparently a kingdom on another world where he lived. Like all good stories, his had battles between good and evil. In fact, he described one in which he had fought against a duke of all things! Why not a prince or a king? That would have been interesting. It was all Alex could do to stop herself laughing at him. The poor man needed help, more help than she could give him. She should have taken Doc up on his offer. Douglas needed full-time supervision in a hospital. His head wound was obviously worse than Doc had thought.

"—I thought we were safe, but that was before I saw your moon and realised I am lost to the world of my birth. Things are very different here, Alex, very different. Where I come from, a Daughter of the Mother would live with her sisters and never alone as you do. I thought you were bringing me to them in your truck, but instead I find a farm not a House of the Mother."

She needed to phone Doc for an ambulance. She made to rise but Douglas took her arm. "Let go," she said stiffly and tested his grip. It was like iron.

"I can prove my words, Sister. I will let you go, but wait before summoning Williams. Yes, I know that was your intention. Who better to deal with a mad man?"

"I don't think you're mad," Alex lied. "You're just confused."

Douglas smiled and opened his free hand to show her what lay there. He held an intricately carved ovoid of stone, or maybe bone, roughly the size of his palm. It was very white, but the carvings were brown and stood out on the white surface.

Alex stared, suddenly fascinated. "What is it?"

"My taufr; it's merely a tool."

"Taufr?"

He shrugged uncomfortably. "A talisman. You do know what a talisman is? You must. I know you have power, and although Daughters of the Mother do things differently, the Pact is not completely forgotten… But of course, I'm a fool! This is another world. You do not know of the Pact."

"I know what a talisman is," she said, humouring him. "But I've never heard of this pact."

"At least that is something," Douglas said with relief. "Touch it."

"Why, what will happen?" she said warily.

"Perhaps nothing. Are you afraid to find out?"

She nodded.

"Good. You should be afraid of touching the unknown, especially a taufr. I swear you will come to no harm this night. Now touch it."

Alex had no reason to trust him, yet somehow she did. Why had she brought him into her home instead of leaving him in Doc's care? Why did she feel uneasy whenever she thought about it? There was something nagging her about the accident, or was it after the accident? She shook off the strange feeling, touched one finger to the taufr, and froze. Her power surged up and into the stone then back into her, bringing with it impossible images of Douglas. He turned and smiled at her as she watched. He waved at her… no, not at her, someone else. These were memories; memories of his home and friends.

A huge black horse trotted forward to greet him, a bearded man wearing a crown frowned at him, and waved him away. Alex saw a castle on an escarpment, banners snapping in the wind, men marching in armour with swords. A beautiful woman screamed in pain, the same woman smiled at him and turned to show him her baby.

Douglas and another man fought in the rain with swords; the other man laughed so hard that Douglas bested him easily. They fell upon the ground laughing and wrestling, their swords forgotten in the mud. Then she saw Douglas holding the man's hand as he died. Douglas screamed like a man on the edge of sanity. She watched Douglas laughing, crying, screaming, fighting… Douglas turning toward her under a night sky with two moons overhead.

You see my surprise now, aren't they beautiful?

"But there are two of them!" Alex gasped.

Three. The hag is yet below the horizon.

"Three moons?"

They're called the Maiden, the Mother, and the Hag. The smallest and brightest is the Maiden, the other you see is the Mother. The Hag is dull and a little smaller than the mother. You will see it just before…

"Before?"

Before I came here.

"Oh."

And there it was, the moment he spoke of. The Hag was high in the sky when the attack came. Douglas fought like a demon, but there were too many. Men fell aside as he cut them down, but always there were more. He narrowly escaped death any number of times, but then a man in black leathers rose up with a bow and Douglas was falling back from a glancing blow to the temple. He fell and splashed into turbulent water. Darkness and pain overwhelmed him, but he struggled to the river's surface. His shoulder smashed into a boulder and he screamed, swallowing more water. He lost his sword as his hand ceased to function. More pain as the river carried him into every rock and boulder it could find.

Alex watched him drag himself out of the river, shivering and hurt, staggering through the woods, climbing a mound surmounted by a stone circle, but ducking and hiding when he spied others already there. She gasped in horror when she saw what he saw, and she despaired with him when the woman died, sacrificed upon a bloody altar. It was like seeing Sharon die all over again. The incantations, the runes, it was all there just as it had been the night Sharon died.

Sacrilege. The traitor used blood to power his magic. See what he holds? An evil thing, created before the Pact. Evil not seen in the kingdom for centuries.

Alex watched as Douglas lunged at Shadowman's back with a dagger. She cheered him on, but before he could snatch the artefact from the man's hand, the runes were complete. A blinding flash of light and both men were tumbling into darkness. More pain and disorientation, a long stumbling walk through countryside, and then she saw the lights of her truck and heard the roar of its engine as it raced toward him.

I thought a demon had come for me.

Alex threw herself away from the bed and broke her contact with the taufr. She sat down hard, unable to save her balance and stared up at Douglas in shock.

"That didn't happen," she gasped. "I didn't see it… it didn't happen… it was a trick! You tricked me!"

"How did I trick you, Sister?" Douglas asked, leaning over the edge of his bed to stare down at her.

"Don't call me that!"

"It was real, you know it was. All you saw happened just as I showed you."

"It's not possible!" she yelled pushing herself backward until her back hit the wall. "It's a trick!"

Douglas sank wearily back and waved a hand at her. "As you will, as you will."

Alex climbed to her feet, feeling strangely guilty for shouting at him. "Do you need anything?"

"Go," Douglas snapped. "I need nothing but rest. Come the morrow, I shall leave you."

Alex bit her lip. She wanted to say that of course, he couldn't leave, he wasn't well enough, but his eyes were already closing. She left him to sleep and quietly closed the door behind her.

Alex sat in the kitchen brooding over what he had told her. It was all fantasy of course. He was mad, and so would she be if she allowed herself to believe it. She glanced guiltily at the phone. Williams would come out if she asked him, even this late he would come, but what would she say? Would she tell him what Douglas told her? Would she pack them both off in an ambulance and forget about them? She should do that. It was the right thing, the *sensible* thing! She tried to make herself get up and use the phone, but suddenly Douglas' blue eyes were in her head looking at her, full of pain. She couldn't do it. She couldn't betray him. He trusted her, and she trusted him—Lady knows why.

Alex thumped the table in frustration feeling tears filling her eyes. The truth was she didn't want to give him up. He was the first person she had met in a long time that she felt comfortable with. She refused to consider it might be more than that. She didn't have to hide herself from him, didn't have to block out his thoughts. That was so rare, so precious. Only Sandy, her best friend from long ago, could compare with Douglas in how easy she felt in their company. He felt comfortable, just comfortable, like an old friend come to visit. She couldn't betray a friend, she mustn't.

Alex frowned. She was being selfish. Douglas needed help, medical help she couldn't supply. He was raving… well not raving precisely. He wasn't violent, but he was delusional. Maybe he just needed rest? She felt hope blossom at the thought, and Douglas' piercing gaze faded from her mind. Yes, she would wait until morning.

She glanced at the phone uncertainly, and Douglas' eyes returned brighter than ever. Yes, she would wait.

* * *

Hours later, Douglas peered into the darkened room that Alex had used to fetch him a glass of water last night. His leg ached dully. That he could stand upon it at all so soon, was entirely due to the marvellous plaster cast Williams had used in place of splints. He knew from experience how bad a break he had suffered. Such had lamed men for life, but Williams was truly a learned man. He had promised the leg would heal as good as new, and Douglas believed him. In his experience, such men as Williams appeared to be were true to their craft and their word. It was not the leg that caused his current distress in any case. It was the state of his bladder he must address at the moment.

He took another hobbling step and found that indeed the little room was an indoor water closet, as he had hoped. A lever on the wall flooded the room with an intense steady light when he used it. He shielded his eyes until they became accustomed to it, and then studied his surroundings. The bath was the same in form to those at home, though this one was not made of copper or any metal he had seen. He wasn't sure it was made of metal at all. Certainly no ordinary blacksmith could make something so large without seams. It was a pale pink in colour, but it wasn't pink granite—it didn't have grains. He rapped a knuckle against it. It didn't ring like metal, and it didn't have the solid feel of stone. It sounded a bit like wood, but it wasn't wood either. Interesting. There was a peculiar arrangement of what could only be faucets at one end. Thank the goddess he recognised something in this crazy world.

He hobbled away from the bath toward a glass cabinet taller than he was. The wonderfully clear glass in Alex's truck was not evident here. The cabinet had very poor glass set in it. He had never seen worse. He couldn't see a blessed thing through it. Another puzzle. Why did her people make such ingenious things, things of almost unnatural quality like the glass in the truck, but then seemingly go out of their way to make poor ones like this cabinet?

Douglas opened the door and was chagrined to find not a cabinet as he had supposed, but another device for washing the body. He was sure that's what it was. The pipes must surely carry water up to the big faucet overhead. He reached out and daringly turned a knob made of crystal. Hot water gushed out of the thing and showered down over his arm. He grinned in delight at the thought of using the wonderful device. It would be like washing in hot rain! He turned the knob back, and tried the other one, already knowing it would make cold water shower down. The blue disk in the centre of the knob seemed a warning, and indeed yes, the water was very cold. He frowned at the pipes and saw that the water would mix if he used both crystals together. A clever way of varying temperature.

Douglas closed the door and found a soft white towel hanging on a rail. He dried his arm and replaced the towel as he found it. The need to empty his bladder was becoming urgent. He looked around for the privy and found something that might do. On the floor was a lidded bowl and above it was a tank with a handle. He lifted the lid and pulled the handle on the tank. Water gushed into the bowl. He didn't know what Alex called it, but he called it good timing.

Douglas sighed as he relieved himself into the bowl. He pulled the handle again and watched his waste sluice away to some unknown destination. Not one to stifle curiosity, he lifted the lid on the water tank and watched it refill. The tank's inner workings revealed themselves to him after a few experimental pulls on the handle. There was nothing very complex in the arrangement; it was a simple pump. He closed the lid, quickly losing interest.

Douglas considered the plaster cast. He wasn't allowed to get it wet, but he couldn't put up with his own stink any longer. He would just have to be careful. He tied a towel around the cast and stepped into the cabinet. A bar of soap lay in a dish attached to one wall. He thoroughly washed his body and tangled hair. The cabinet filled with steam while he stood under the artificial rain shower. It felt wonderful to be clean again, and he was tempted to linger, but he quashed the impulse. The cast looked none the worse for his quick wash, but he would not chance staying longer. He dried himself and pulled on his filthy clothes. It seemed a shame to undo all his work with dirty clothing, but he had no others. His boots were out of the question. He would go unshod.

By the time he had dressed the sun was well up, but Alex's door remained firmly closed—not a sound came from her direction. This was her house; he dare not intrude to waken her, yet he was reluctant to leave without word. He stifled his impatience and dropped his boots beside the door before stepping outside. He would wait to take his leave of her. With nothing else to do, he chose to explore. Progress would be slow, hobbling as he was, but the world entire was new. There would be much to see even here close to the Yorke Place.

"A strange name," he mused as he made his way to the stable to investigate its contents.

Douglas found two horses, neither animal was fit for war, but then this was a farm. The beasts were probably used to pull a cart or plough. They were affectionate rogues; both of them greeted him by reaching their heads over the stall doors. He patted both and gave them each a scoop of oats from the bin just inside the door. While they munched happily, he scouted the stable but there was nothing to see. The saddles were different from the ones he was used to, but not enough to interest him. The tools hanging on the wall were peculiar, but he wasn't a craftsman to have an interest in such things.

He led the horses one at a time out of the stable and into

the paddock. He found a currycomb and thought Alex might appreciate it if he worked off a little of his debt by grooming them. He worked on the grey first and grinned when the other brute pushed him in the back. She was impatient and wanted the same treatment.

It was like that Alex found him. She was wearing her blue trousers that clung to her hips and were so tight they might have been painted on, and above that a loose fitting bright red shirt that left her midriff bare. The flash of pale skin just above her belt mesmerised him, and he had to force his eyes away. She wore her long blonde hair in a single thick braid that reached between her shoulder blades.

"His name is Smokey," Alex said leaning upon the rail.

"What?"

"The grey. His name's Smokey."

"And the roan?" he said, gesturing with the brush at the other animal.

"Nuisance."

He snorted. "Good name for him."

Alex grinned. "He's been pestering you, hasn't he?"

Douglas smiled and nodded. "I was waiting for you to rise. I didn't want to leave without saying good-bye."

"You can't go!" Alex gasped. "I mean, are you sure you're well enough?"

"I can travel." He grimaced. "Slowly."

"But where will you go?"

He shrugged, but the thought was a concern. "I don't know, but eventually home. I have to find that cursed... forgive me. I have to find Karel, the man that opened the gate, and force him to take us back. We don't belong here."

Alex frowned. "I'm sorry about the way I reacted last night. It was a lot to take in. You have to understand something, Douglas. There's no such thing as magic here. I mean there is magic, but it's nothing like what you seem to mean."

Douglas snorted in disbelief. "Don't talk rot. You're a witch,

Alex. You have power, I've felt it. Of course there is magic."

Alex shook her head tiredly. "I don't want to argue with you. Just believe me when I say that I'm not a witch as you mean the word. Some have called me that, but I'm not. I can do things sometimes, strange things, but I don't cast spells. I can't. What I do is just something science has yet to explain. If you go telling people that you can work magic, they'll think you're crazy."

He frowned. She sounded sincere but how could he believe her? "What magic is this *science* you speak of?"

"No magic at all. Science is… well it's the knowledge of how things work. Like… oh hell," she muttered. "Like how to work metal into horseshoes, or how to build a bridge and know it won't fall down even when the river is at its height."

Douglas brightened, at last something he understood. "You speak of the artisan's secrets."

"If you mean people who make things, then yes, sort of. Science is how artisans learned how to do the things they do."

Douglas shook his head. She had misunderstood him. "The secrets are passed down from father to son. Some do become common knowledge through familiarity, but most are held tight to the chest and closely guarded. Guild artificers have killed to keep their secrets."

"But there had to be a first time for everything they make. You like my truck right?"

He wouldn't go that far. "It's interesting."

"There are lots of moving parts to make it go. Each one had to be designed. It took science to design them, and science to put them all together. Now do you see?"

He looked at the truck and then at Alex. "No."

"Oh hell," Alex muttered.

Douglas thought she might try again to make her implausible point, but another truck arrived. It didn't look like Alex's truck, but it had unmistakable similarities. It was lower to the ground, and faster looking, with markings on its side.

On its roof, there was a red glass dome.

"Oh bloody hell," Alex muttered then said, "Let me do the talking." She marched across the yard to meet the man climbing out of the truck. "Tomas! You brought the map?"

Tomas was holding a package of paper and frowning at Douglas who awkwardly climbed over the fence. "I brought it. Who is your friend?"

"Oh, that's Douglas. Just in from Portland. Didn't I mention he was visiting?"

"Portland, huh?" Tomas looked Douglas up and down. He frowned at the cast and dirty bare feet. "Quite a trip."

Douglas nodded. "A very distant land, yes."

Alex winced.

"I'm Sheriff Edwards," Tomas said holding out his hand.

Douglas clasped it and they shook. "Honoured to meet you, sir. I am Douglas of… Portland."

"No last name?"

Alex began to answer for him, but Douglas saw no harm in the question. "Skeldon. Douglas Skeldon is my name, sir."

"Skeldon," Tomas said, rolling the name on his tongue as if trying to taste it. "A good friend are you?"

"Yes," Alex said at the same time as Douglas' "I hope so."

"Where did you meet?"

"On the road," Douglas said.

Alex jumped in. "He means we met on a road trip. I was vacationing last year and we bumped into each other outside a theatre. I can't remember the name of the play now. What was it Doug?"

Douglas looked at her uncertainly and thought she shook her head slightly. "I can't remember either. It wasn't very good I seem to recall."

Tomas looked from Alex to Douglas. "Is that right?" He said slowly, not sounding convinced. "Well, I'm glad to see that Alex has some company out here. With what's been going on, I feel better knowing she's not alone."

"Might I enquire what has been going on?" Douglas asked, wondering at the concern in the newcomer's face.

"She didn't tell you?"

"I arrived quite unexpectedly," he said and Alex winced again. He could think of no reason for it. "If it's not a secret, perhaps you…?"

"No secret. The whole damn county knows we've had a bunch of killings."

"Murdered?"

Tomas nodded. "That's right, Mr. Skeldon, murdered. Alex has been trying to help. You know what she can do?"

"Some," he said. Alex pretended she was not a Daughter of the Mother, a witch, but he knew different. He could feel her power.

Tomas waved the package he carried in the air. "She saw some kind of ritual, and the one responsible is still at large. I've been trying to persuade her to come into town, but she won't let me do my job and protect her."

A ritual murder. Blood magic, here?

Douglas shifted uneasily. "You believe this man might come here?"

"It's possible. A lot of people know she helped us."

Alex glared at Tomas. "I can take care of myself. Don't start, just don't start, okay?"

"You should let Lord Tomas protect you," Douglas said.

"No! I'm not letting either of you persuade me to leave my home. I told Tomas and now I'm telling you, I won't go!"

"She's real stubborn," Tomas confided.

Douglas nodded. "I'm coming to realise that."

"About the map," Tomas said reaching into the package he held and pulling out a map. He passed it to Alex. "Think you can do something with it?"

Alex frowned at it and shook her head. "I don't know. I'll try. Let's go inside." She led the way.

"What happened to the leg?" Tomas asked as they made

their way to the house.

Douglas shrugged. "Broke it. I was hit by a truck, but it will heal well I'm told."

"Glad to hear it." Tomas glanced behind him at Alex's truck for a brief moment. "You want help up the steps?"

"I can manage, sir, thank you."

Alex led them into the kitchen and they seated themselves around the table. Douglas found much in the room to catch his eye, but by far the most interesting was Alex herself. She spread the map upon the table and sat before it. Early morning sunlight spilled through the windows and shone upon her face as she closed her eyes. One hand hovered over the map, the other lay flat upon the table beside it. Tomas leaned forward in expectation.

Douglas simply watched in puzzlement as Alex used her magic. How could she say there was no magic when it spilled out of her like a flood with every breath? He watched her doing something, felt it brush past him like the memory of a lover's kiss, and had no idea what she was trying to do. She frowned in concentration, and her hand moved back and forth over the map with no obvious purpose in doing so. Oh, he knew Tomas wanted her to find something, why else use a map? But Alex hadn't conjured a location spell, nor was she using witch sense as far as he could tell. Being a man it was hard for him, but he had seen other Daughters of the Mother use it. Alex didn't feel cold and distant as they had. She felt warm and alive like summer, full to bursting with life and power. It was very... *disturbing*.

Douglas shifted uncomfortably in his seat as certain parts of his body reacted fiercely. He reached beneath the table and made himself more comfortable, all the while thinking about a swim in frigid water. His manhood shrivelled at the thought.

"What's she doing?" he asked quietly and Alex frowned.

"She said..." Tomas lowered his voice. "She told me that she felt the one we're looking for is south of the town. I've had my boys looking everywhere we can think of, but we found squat. I'm hoping she might be able to point him out on the map."

"And you believe she can do this?"

Tomas looked embarrassed. "I don't know. I sure hope so."

"Is the map magic in some manner?"

"Nope!" Alex burst out in a rush and cutting Douglas off. "Nothing comes to me. I'm sorry, Tomas. I can't help you."

Douglas knew a way that might work. "Alex, I could show—"

Alex kicked his good leg under the table and Tomas frowned suspiciously. "It was a long shot, Doug. We thought it worth a try, but neither of us expected it to work. Right, Tomas?"

"It *was* a long shot, but I've got to be honest, I doubt we'll find the killer without more long shots, and you know what that means."

"Another body," Alex whispered.

"It's how things work," Tomas said. "He made some mistakes last time, but before we could exploit them and find his accomplice, the killer took him out to shut him up." He opened the package he had brought and spilled its contents—pictures—onto the table. He pushed them toward Alex. "Recognise anything?"

"This is the car I saw."

"Right. And this one?" Tomas said, pointing to another picture.

"The driver? I heard him mostly, it was dark." She looked through the other pictures stopping to study each one. "I did see him better that time in the morgue when he visited Currie."

Tomas reached out and tapped one of them with a finger. "This guy owned the car, right enough. Stupid to use his own, but maybe not. If not for you, we wouldn't have known what to look for."

Douglas craned his neck, trying to see what Alex held, and she passed the pictures to him. They were made of paper. At least he thought they were. They were perfectly smooth and shiny. No artist he had ever heard of could draw something so fine as the pictures displayed on one side of each sheet. More of Alex's science magic, it must be.

One picture was of a truck, but Tomas said *car*. So there were different sorts. Small ones were *cars*. The second picture was of a dead man. He didn't recognise anything except that the man was dead. He knew dead when he saw it. Other pictures were of a house and its surroundings. It was one of these that made him snarl in hate. It showed the *car* again from a different angle. In the background there were people watching and held back by a rope barrier. He recognised one of them.

Alex noticed his sudden tension. "Doug, are you all right?" Her eyes slid sideways to Tomas in warning. "Do you need another painkiller?"

"I… yes, the leg is paining me."

Tomas took back the pictures and hid them away in the brown paper sleeve they came in. He began folding the map. "I should be going."

Alex filled a glass with water. She handed it and a painkiller to Douglas. He didn't need one but dutifully swallowed it and chased it with water. He couldn't take his eyes from what Tomas held.

"I'm sorry I couldn't help." Alex accompanied Tomas to the door and opened it for him. "Wait, would it be all right if I kept the map and photos? I could try again later and call you."

Tomas hesitated, but he passed the package across. "Call me the moment you think you have something. Day or night. The *instant*, hear me?"

"I will. The second I know something. I promise."

Tomas nodded. "Nice to have met you, Doug. Look after our Alex, hear?"

"I hear most clearly. No harm will befall her, you have my word."

Tomas nodded again and left.

* * *

7~Betrayal

Alex watched Tomas drive away then rejoined Douglas in the kitchen. "He's suspicious. He noticed your slip, Doug, don't think he didn't."

Douglas frowned. "Why must I lie to him? I do not like to tell untruths if I can avoid it."

"Neither do I, but you can't tell him what you told me. First, he won't believe you. Second, you're a stranger, and it's a really bad time to be a stranger around here. Tomas is looking for a murderer. Any strangers are going to be on his list of suspects. He accepted you because I pretended to know you. If not for that, I guarantee he would have taken you in for questioning."

"I've done nothing," Douglas protested.

Alex patted his hand where it lay upon the table. "I know you're not the one he's looking for, Doug. The murderer's presence is like a shadow on the web, slimy and evil. You're nothing like him. I trust you, but you have to trust me when I say you cannot tell Tomas what you told me last night."

"I do trust you, Alex."

Alex flushed at his appreciative stare. "Well, okay then. We need to get you a few things—clothes and stuff. I haven't anything here that will fit. We need to go into town for that. Have you decided where you'll go after?"

Douglas cocked his head at her. "All I know of your world I have learned from you, Alex. Tell me where I should go. Who will help me return to my own world?"

She sighed. Not this again. "Listen, you know what I think about that."

"But it's the truth. What would convince you? Tell me, and I will do it."

"You can't prove the impossible!"

"Try me."

Alex frowned. She had witnessed some very strange things in her life. Hell, *she* was a very strange thing compared with most people! What if he really did come from another world? No, it wasn't possible. There was no such thing as magic like he described, even practicing witches would agree with her on that, and she knew quite a few. Magical gates that led to other worlds were pure fantasy. Wonderful as magic like that would be, it was just not possible. It was all a trick.

Alex frowned as something else occurred to her. "How come you speak English?"

Douglas avoided her eyes. "What has that got to do with anything?"

"If you really come from another world, you shouldn't speak my language."

"Alex, I…" Douglas looked away and muttered something under his breath. "I won't lie to you. You're right, I did trick you."

"Ha! I knew it couldn't have been real. I knew it was some kind of trick—"

"You're wrong!" Douglas snarled. "What you saw was real. I swear it, Alex. On my honour I swear it, but I did take advantage of you. I used the opportunity to enter your mind and learn your language when you touched my taufr last night. I'm sorry; I didn't know what else to do."

Alex frowned in puzzlement. "But you spoke to me before that—on the road and in the hospital."

Douglas grimaced. "I knew I didn't understand your tongue the moment you opened your mouth, Alex. I cast a spell to make you understand my words and did the same with Williams at the hospital, but I couldn't keep using it forever. You would have noticed. I took advantage of your trust last night. I'm sorry."

Alex stared at him. She didn't know him well enough to feel betrayed, but that's how she felt. She had helped him, trusted him, and he had rummaged around in her head without her permission. He had violated her mind, her privacy. The most intimate details of her life had been open to him. It was intolerable!

"You *bastard.*"

Douglas' face hardened. "Contrary to popular belief, lady, I am no bastard."

"What else did you do to me last night?"

"I don't—"

"There's something else, isn't there? I know it, I *feel* it! Why did I bring you home last night? You're a stranger. It's crazy to trust you, but I do… I did." She shook her head in confusion. "Why didn't I leave you with Doc Williams? You could be anyone, even a murderer for all I know!"

Douglas flinched.

"Tell me!"

Douglas shook his head silently.

"Answer me, or Lady help me I'll call Tomas and make him put you behind bars!"

"I did nothing to harm you," Douglas protested. "You have my word."

"Your *word,*" Alex sneered, shaking with anger. "What good is that, huh? You tell me. What good is your word when you've already abused my trust?"

Douglas' shoulders slumped. "You're right. What I did was

wrong, I admit it, but I was desperate. Think for a minute. Put yourself in my place. This is not my world."

Alex would have broken in then, but he bulled ahead.

"I know you don't believe me, but it's the truth. I swear by the Goddess and my powers. May she strike me dead if I lie. I was born the middle son of Conall and Rowena—the Duke and Duchess of Dun'Morgan. I was raised in Skeldon Castle in the west of Inari, and found myself here by the foulest use of magic as you saw last night. All this do I swear on my life and powers, Goddess bear witness!"

He sounded so damned sincere, but did that make what he said true? Alex had no doubt he believed his own story, but he might be deluded. For all she knew he might have escaped from a mental institution.

"What did you do to me? And no lies this time."

Douglas nodded. "No lies then. I used a spell—little more than a trick really—to make you understand my words. Had you listened closely, you would have realised I wasn't speaking English. The other spell…"

"Go on."

Douglas sighed glumly. "I compelled you to aid me, to trust me like an old friend—*I had no choice, Alex!* You must believe me. More than my life depends upon my returning home as quickly as may be. I needed your help badly. I still do. All I know of this world I have learned from you."

"Earth. It's called Earth… the world I mean," she said mulling over his story.

Douglas believed his mad story, but no matter how much she wanted to, she did not. The realisation that she *did* want to believe him gave her pause. Was her life so bad then?

"I beg your forgiveness, lady. Do you give it?"

Alex shook her head and Douglas' face fell. "Undo what you did, and I may still help you."

His face brightened and Alex shifted uncomfortably. He had only done to her what she had done to others. Like Meeks.

She had compelled Meeks to go on an errand for her. It wasn't the first time she had done something like that, and she was honest enough to admit it wouldn't be the last.

It's not the same thing.

Wasn't it? Meeks hadn't been hurt, and neither was she when Douglas used compulsion upon her. She would be a hypocrite of the worst order to punish him for doing as she had done so many times.

I don't care! The bastard was in my head. He might have seen how she felt about him.

Her face reddened at the thought.

Douglas must have taken her reaction as evidence of growing anger, because he hastily retrieved his taufr and touched it to her forehead. A shiver past through her, but when he stepped back, she felt no different. She frowned and considered what had happened. Did she believe Douglas' story now? No, but she still believed that he believed it. That was no help. Did she trust him? Not unreservedly, no, but she didn't completely mistrust him either. He didn't feel like an old friend, but neither did he feel like an enemy. He was a stranger, a blank slate to her. As it should be for someone she had only just met.

"I don't feel much different."

Douglas nodded. "That's the problem with compulsions, they wear off over time. If I hadn't removed it, it would have been completely gone by tomorrow. The next day at the latest."

That felt right to her. When she *pushed* someone, it never had a lasting effect. "I still don't believe your story."

"But—"

Alex raised a hand. "I believe that you believe it."

"Forgive me if I'm not much comforted, lady. You think me either a deluded fool or a madman. I'm not sure which is worse."

Alex grinned at his sour tone, but then frowned. How

could she believe anything he said now? There was only one way she could think of, but it made her uneasy. What if he had told her the truth, what then?

"Show me some magic and maybe, *maybe*, I'll believe you."

"Maybe?" Douglas smiled wryly. "You hedge your bets worse than a merchant!"

"Show me something, and then we'll see."

"What sort of thing?"

"Any sort of thing! Goddess, Doug, just show me something simple."

Douglas sighed in frustration. "But you will say it was a trick like last night."

"Then make it something I won't say is a trick… oh wait a minute, wait a minute! I see what you're doing now. You can't do it, can you?"

Douglas scowled. "Anything can be dismissed by someone not willing to believe, Alex."

"That someone isn't me. I would love to believe your magic is real, I really would, but I can't take it on faith. I'm not made that way. You'll have to prove it to me."

"But you just saw me… ah, you want something you can see and touch?"

Alex nodded. "Something simple."

Douglas frowned. "Something simple she says, something simple. Sit in that chair and don't move."

"Why?" Alex said, eyeing the chair warily. "What are you going to do?"

Douglas growled something under his breath. "Just do it, or are you too frightened to know the truth?"

"I already know the truth, remember?"

"No, you only think you do." Douglas pulled his taufr from the little leather pouch on his belt.

Alex sat nervously in her chair and watched Douglas intently. He cupped the talisman in both hands and scowled at it furiously.

"There. Satisfied?"

"What did you do?"

Douglas smirked. "Look down."

Alex looked down and yelled. The chair started to wobble from her sudden movement, and she had to grab the arms to stop herself falling. The chair, with her on it, floated on a cushion of nothing. A couple more feet and her head would have bumped the ceiling!

She waved her hands above her head, searching for invisible wires, and then all round the floating chair. She couldn't reach beneath it, but she doubted there was anything to find. She carefully jumped down to the floor and stared up at the floating chair. Douglas laughed so hard, she thought he might do himself permanent harm.

"Oh, my Lady, you did it!" Alex said in stunned delight.

"Yes."

"But you did it!"

"Yes, I know, Alex. It's a very simple spell—one that apprentices learn for practice. You did say that you wanted simple."

Alex stared up in wonder. "But it's floating on nothing!"

He shook his head. "It's floating on air. There's a difference."

"What difference? It's floating!"

"Sit down, Alex, and I'll explain a few things."

Alex couldn't keep her eyes off the chair. She fumbled behind her for another one and sat. Reaching up to the chair leg closest to her, she nudged it gently. The chair spun slowly. As it turned, her entire world changed. She felt it realigning, shifting into a new pattern where overt magic not only could exist, but emphatically did. None of her studies could have prepared her for it. Years of studying the paranormal, years of studying Wicca, years of associating with men and woman who practiced the Craft and called themselves witches, and none of it had prepared her for the sheer wonder of it. This wasn't wishful thinking, or hysteria, or science misunderstood, this was… magic!

Alex grinned and nudged the chair again.

"…and called it levitation. Alex?"

"What?"

"Are you listening to me?"

"It's floating," she said, then frowned worriedly. "Do you know what this means?"

Douglas shrugged. "That I was telling the truth?"

"Yes!"

"I told you I was."

"Yes, but this is marvellous. Can you teach me?" she said eagerly.

"I don't know. Perhaps. You have to realise that men and women are different, Alex. What works for one, doesn't always work for the other."

"Can you bring it down?"

"Easily."

"Show me," she said and Douglas did.

When the chair was back on the floor, she picked it up. It felt the same as before. It was no lighter than it had been and looked the same. She turned it over and felt the underside of the seat. The short hairs on her arm lifted, but she put that down to the excitement.

"It's exactly the same as the others."

Douglas nodded. "What did you expect?"

Alex shrugged. "I don't know. For it to be lighter maybe."

"The spell doesn't work that way. I simply used the air below the chair to lift it."

"Air."

"Right," Douglas said.

"Air used to lift things," she mused and frowned. "Air pressure, maybe?"

"What?"

"I said air pressure. My people have learned that certain shapes, called airfoils, can lift heavy weights when moved through the air at speed. It's just a difference in air pressure."

Douglas' eyes were glazed. "Oh."

She was boring him, and airfoils didn't explain a floating chair anyway. It was magic! She grinned at Douglas, but her delight drained away as she remembered why they were doing this. "I guess I owe you an apology for not believing you last night."

Douglas waved that away. "It matters not."

"It does, though. I was determined not to believe you. I'm sorry, Douglas."

"For what?"

"For everything—hitting you with the truck, doubting you, thinking you were mad. I of all people should have been willing to at least hear you out, but instead I called it a trick and dismissed it. You know I have this thing inside me—don't call it magic."

Douglas clamped his mouth shut, protest unspoken.

"I have this thing, this power, and I used it to help Tomas. I saw something that should have made me believe you."

"Saw what?"

Alex closed her eyes briefly, suddenly looking grave. "I saw a woman horribly murdered."

"The ritual Lord Tomas spoke of?"

She shook her head. "He's not a lord; we don't have lords in this country. Tomas is our sheriff... law man?"

"Ah! I understand. He's a thief-catcher."

"Well, he does catch thieves, that's true, but he does more than that. He and his men are responsible for catching anyone who commits any kind of crime within his jurisdiction. A friend of mine works with Tomas. She asked me to help her. Tomas didn't like it—he's uncomfortable with things he doesn't understand—but he's desperate to find the killer before another murder happens."

"I understand, but you mentioned a ritual."

Alex grimaced. "I saw the murder. A man carved runes into the victim while she was still alive and then killed her. Her heart and eyes were missing when Jenn found her."

Douglas spat a vile oath and then looked up, red-faced. "Excuse me, Lady Alex, I forgot myself. What you describe is an abomination to my people."

"It was the same as you showed me in the vision."

"Not quite, lady, but close. The vision… I should tell you that what you call a vision was in fact a memory; my memory. A vision is an entirely different thing."

Alex leaned forward eagerly. "How is it different?"

"Most people believe that visions are sent by the Mother Goddess to her chosen—*only* to her chosen. I know this to be false. They would call me heretic for saying that, but I know what is true."

"And what *is* true?"

"That visions are sent by the Goddess to anyone she deems worthy." He looked down. "Even a man."

"How do you know?"

"She sent one to me," Douglas said quietly looking away, as if fearing her censure.

"What was it?"

Douglas' eyes shot back to hold hers. "You believe me?"

"Of course I believe you if you say it. Why shouldn't I?"

Douglas grinned. "You're a very contrary person, Alex. You know that surely?"

She laughed. "I've always thought of myself as pretty straightforward."

"That you are not. You don't believe the most ordinary things about my world—"

"Hey! I apologised for that already."

"—and then you say that you believe the things my people would find the most *un*believable." Douglas shook his head, smiling ruefully. "If I confessed to my people what I have to you, they would think me deluded at best and pity me for believing it. At worst... well, it's best not to contemplate the worst that could happen. Suffice it to say, I would never confess my belief to anyone but you—not even to the most loyal friend I have."

"Why say it to me then?"

Douglas shrugged. "I don't know, but I think my secret is safe with you. Besides, it doesn't matter now. This is another world vastly removed from mine. How can what I say here hurt me there?"

Alex shook her head. "Beats me. You say the ritual you showed me was different from the one I saw before. How was it different?"

Douglas frowned in thought and drew meaningless patterns with a finger upon the tabletop. "Certain magics—dark magics—require blood. It's an *absolute* requirement, not a preference. The spell will not work without it. A death is not always necessary, but those who scruple to use such filthy magics rarely worry about killing the innocent. Blood magic of any kind is considered evil—even seemingly innocent uses."

"Are there innocent uses?"

Douglas nodded. "I could prick my finger and use my own blood to power a spell, and it would be much stronger than the same spell created without using blood. I could call a spark to light my campfire let's say, but if I use blood, a flame strong enough to burn a house to the ground could result. You see? Anything that sacrifices bodily essence will always have a stronger effect. It doesn't even have to be blood. I could use breath or even my spittle—I have offended you."

Alex had been shaking her head in fascination. "No, no. I'm not easily offended. It's just that all this takes some getting used to. Does the sacrifice have to be animate?"

"By that you mean it must come from a living being?"

"Yes."

"It's a matter of degree," Douglas hedged. "Wine makes

a good sacrifice for certain spells, especially if the spell was intended to help the vines in a vineyard grow. Gold would be my preference for a spell designed to find a lost valuable. You see?"

Alex nodded. "You try to match the sacrifice with what the spell is intended to do."

"All the best spells are made that way. Spells that sacrifice bodily essence are the strongest, though as I said, they aren't always the most suitable. Blood is a strong sacrifice. Blood resulting in death stronger still, and…"

"And?"

Douglas hesitated. "The strongest of all is the power released by the destruction of a soul."

Alex felt the blood drain from her face. "That's what I saw, isn't it?"

"I didn't see what you saw, but I fear so."

"Are you telling me that not only did he kill poor Sharon, he destroyed her soul too?"

"Yes." Douglas shrugged. "Probably."

"But why?! Why do that?"

"I'm guessing, but I think he needed more power to open the gate from this side. Magic feels weaker here; mine does at least. He probably couldn't work his spell without the sacrifice of a soul."

Alex nodded thoughtfully. That made about as much sense as anything else she had thought of. "Is it because you don't belong here?"

"I'm not sure, but maybe. Your magic feels strong to me, but then I'm a weak mage in any world. Your power is constantly flowing out of you. This house is thick with it."

Alex grimaced. "I've never understood what I do. I can't control it or stop it."

"But surely you have been trained?"

She laughed bitterly. "I told you before. Magic, real magic like yours, doesn't exist here. Who could teach me about what does not exist?"

Douglas stared at Alex for a long moment as if unable to believe what she had told him. He reached for her hand. "You don't even know how to shield, do you?"

Alex shrugged, but kept his hand in hers. She liked the feeling of connection that came with his warmth. "If I understand what you mean by shielding, then I guess not. What I do sounds completely different. I've studied with Wiccans—you would say witches—who tried to help me, but apart from learning about the Goddess and the God, I learned nothing to help my condition. You're the only person who can touch me without triggering my *gift*," she said bitterly.

"That's because I'm using my magic to counter yours. I've been doing it all along. Don't hate your power, Alex. It would be like hating yourself. You only need to be taught how to control it."

"*Can* you teach me?"

Douglas hesitated but then shook his head. "Daughters of the Mother do things differently. I could show you what I know, but the chances are it wouldn't work properly or even at all. Men shield themselves by building walls in their minds."

"I do that!" she said excitedly, but then she hedged. "Sort of. I imagine myself as a pillar of rock and everyone's thoughts as the sea. The sea is powerful, but I am rock. Ever there, ever strong."

"That's a man's technique. I'm not surprised you cannot bear another's touch. Witches have other ways, powerful ways to protect themselves. Women's secrets are not for men. You need your sisters to teach you, but you say there are none here."

"You don't know how they do it?"

"No man does, Alex. I'm sorry."

Alex's shoulders slumped in defeat.

* * *

8~Revelations

Douglas felt Alex's disappointment in him keenly. He would have done anything to help her, but he didn't have the knowledge. He was a very poor wizard, and knew only bits and pieces of magic. She needed the support of her sisters, but they weren't to be found here. Without them, she would be doomed to live a half life. He had heard stories of witches succumbing to madness or even death for want of proper training. The thought of something of the sort happening to Alex was unbearable.

"I got this for you. It was obvious you wanted it." Alex spilled the contents of Tomas' packet on the table. "What did you see?"

He rummaged through the pictures until he found the one he wanted and stabbed a finger down, nailing the image of his enemy. "This man. I know this man." Alex rested a hand upon his shoulder and leaned down beside him. "Mardus is Wallace's man."

"From…?"

"My world, yes."

"But he's not the killer," Alex protested. "I don't recognise his face."

Douglas picked up the picture and glared at it. "Mardus may not be the killer you seek, but he is one nonetheless. I doubt he has changed his ways since coming here. Believe me, he's dangerous."

Alex nodded. "I believe you. How did he get here? He didn't come with you, did he?"

Douglas frowned. He hadn't considered that. "No, he wasn't at the circle of Velkomen. He didn't come through with me."

"In that case the question becomes, when did he get here and why did he come? What's he after?"

"I don't know."

Alex abruptly left to enter another room. When she returned, she held some kind of weapon. He had never seen anything like it, but he knew a weapon when he saw one. It had a deadly looking efficiency, and Alex handled it with care.

"I hope you don't plan on using that thing, whatever it is, on me," he said trying to see how it might work.

Alex held up the weapon for Douglas' inspection. "This is a 40 calibre semi-automatic handgun. A friend got it for me. It's the same as the police use in Los Angeles, and I know how to use it. If this Mardus character comes here intending mischief, he will regret it."

"A *handgun?* How does it work?"

"Well, it's… I guess it's like a bow?" Alex said, not sounding very sure about the comparison.

Douglas regarded the thing doubtfully. "That's a bow? It looks nothing like one, not even a crossbow."

"I said it's *like* a bow, not that it was one. Come outside and I'll show you how it works."

Douglas followed Alex outside and watched her lean a wooden post against the bales of straw piled up to one side of the stable. She came back to join him, did something with the *handgun*, and took a bent-kneed stance. She held the weapon in both hands and squeezed the trigger.

Crack! Crack! Crack!

Douglas jumped at the sound. Alex did something to her weapon and beckoned him to follow her back to the post.

"There, see? It throws tiny metal arrows called bullets. That's why I said it's like a bow."

He fingered the splintered holes in the post. "Bullets. Like a shepherd boy's sling."

"I suppose." Alex shrugged. "The bullets come out very fast. If I hit Mardus with this, he would most likely have a hole right through him. He definitely won't like it."

What a lovely thought, it brightened Douglas' day just imagining it. "No, I don't suppose he would. Can I try?"

"Sure. Let me show you how it works."

Douglas watched intently as Alex removed a part of the gun she called the magazine and showed him the bullets. She quickly reloaded the magazine and replaced it in the gun. She worked the part that she called the slide, and clicked on the safety.

"Must I always work the slide before pulling the trigger?"

Alex shook her head. "That's why this kind of gun is called an automatic. After loading, you have to work the slide to get the first bullet into position, but after that you don't have to. When the gun is fired, some of the... *force* that pushes the bullet out loads the next one." She handed the gun to him. "Don't forget the safety, and try to squeeze the trigger. If you jerk it you'll miss."

Douglas aimed carefully at the post and pulled the trigger. The gun leapt in his fist. He shook his tingling hand; it felt a little numb. The sensation faded rapidly leaving behind it a dull ache in his wrist. He had no idea where the bullet had gone, but it wasn't into the post.

Alex patted his shoulder. "You weren't ready for the recoil. Don't worry about missing, the straw will catch them."

Douglas tried again. This time splinters flew from the top edge of the post. With Alex muttering encouragement, he continued firing until the slide locked open. He passed the gun back to Alex and went to inspect the post. Each of his shots was closer than the last to his aim point. A little more practice and he would be hitting what he aimed at consistently.

"Quick and easy to learn." He frowned uneasily. "This could be bad."

"Bad?"

"I was just imagining Mardus learning to use one of your guns."

Alex cocked her head and frowned at him. "Why would he bother? He has magic, doesn't he?"

"What makes you say that?"

"Well I thought... doesn't he have magic like you?"

He shook his head. "Not as far as I know. Mardus is a captain in Wallace's guard. He's nothing more than that. It was Karel's spell that brought me here. He's known in Inari as a great wizard with a dark reputation. He will do anything, no matter how foul, as long as the price is right. The rumours say the Guild ejected him years ago when he attempted to steal something from the vaults below the Guild Hall at Hardenburg. Whatever the truth, the Guild withdrew its protection and put a price on his head. No one has lived long enough to collect it."

Alex began reloading the gun's magazine. "He sounds like my Shadowman, the one Tomas is after."

"If he is, Tomas would do well to stay away. I can't stress enough how dangerous Karel is, Alex. Mardus would simply kill you, but Karel would do worse. He would torment you until you begged for death and enjoy doing it."

Alex shuddered. "Is there any way you can find Karel or Mardus? If we can set the cops on them, we'll be safe."

There was one way, but he hesitated to reveal it. No matter how much Karel deserved death, Douglas needed him alive to get home. "There might be, but I can't let Tomas kill or capture Karel. Please understand, Alex, I need to get home with what

I've learned of Wallace's plans. Tomas can have Mardus and his men, and welcome to them, but I need Karel to get back. Even if Tomas could catch Karel, which I seriously doubt, he could never hold him. It would take Guild rune speakers to bind him."

"Rune speakers," Alex muttered. "Silly me."

Douglas took her hand and squeezed it gently. "This is all new to you, I know, but just think what could happen should Karel be captured and still able to use his magic."

Alex nodded and squeezed his hand in return. "I understand. Tell me what you need and I'll get it for you."

"I need you, mostly."

"Me? What can I do?"

Douglas smiled. "You'd be surprised. With training you would give the Reverend Mother herself pause, but we haven't time for that. My magic has always been weak, Alex. I know less than a hedge wizard, but at least what I know works. In this world, my magic feels weaker than ever. I'm not sure that anything I try will work here. I need your strength for the spell."

"I'll help," Alex said eagerly. "Just tell me what to do."

Douglas smiled, but inside he cringed. It was appalling how easily she put herself in his hands. He would never harm her, but the same could not be said for Karel and others he had met. What if, instead of him, she had struck Karel that night? The consequences didn't bear thinking about.

He turned back toward the house. "Let's go inside and I'll explain what we'll need."

Alex helped him back inside to the kitchen.

Douglas picked up the picture of Mardus from the table again and frowned worriedly. The spell needed a focus and all he had was this picture made with Alex's science magic. He had no way to know if such a focus would work. It should; spells depended upon the caster's ability to symbolise one thing with another. Like a bowl of salt used to represent earth, or incense to represent air. The connection between them was in the spell caster's mind. As long as he believed in the connection between Mardus' image and Mardus himself, it should work.

He slumped onto a chair with his leg stuck out to one side of the table. "This picture will be the focus for the spell," he said, trying to sound confident. "We will also need salt for the circle, four bowls, four candles—"

"Wait, let me get a pen. I want to write this down," Alex said over her shoulder as she went into the other room.

Douglas waited for her to return with pen and paper before continuing. "I will need amber for strength, amethyst to increase awareness, and maybe some malachite for protection from danger. I'm not sure it will help against someone like Karel, but it can't hurt. Obsidian would be good if you can get it. I like to use it when divining if I can. It's not essential, but I would feel better if we had some."

Alex nodded as she made her notes. "I'll try. What about an athame?"

Douglas pursed his lips as he considered an athame. He had lost his sword in the fight on the bridge, and rued the loss more than ever now. He had always used it as his athame. "I lost my sword when I fell into the river. I'll need something to replace it."

"Swords aren't that common here, Douglas. I know some people who could probably get me one if I asked, or at least lend me one. Does it have to be a sword—couldn't you use a ritual knife?"

He grimaced. "To be honest I would prefer a sword. Daughters of the Mother would never agree with me—they have strong views regarding bloodletting of any kind, and especially where magic is concerned. I never had anything bad happen when using my sword as an athame, but I always purified it before working magic just in case." He shrugged uncomfortably. "You can't be too careful where magic is concerned."

"All Daughters of the Mother are witches?"

He nodded firmly. "All."

"And they don't like using swords?"

"They believe the sword taints any magic it comes into contact with, because it's too closely linked with battle and death. Symbols are especially important where magic is concerned."

Alex nodded thoughtfully. "That's interesting."

"Why?"

"I know a couple of Wiccans who prefer to use a sword. Athames are never used to draw blood, and most people use a blunted knife, but swords are okay here."

Douglas grinned. "That's probably because your people use other weapons to kill their enemies. If someone wanted to use a gun for their athame, I'd wager it would cause a fuss."

Alex grinned back. "It certainly would!" She frowned as something else occurred to her. "There are places that sell swords. There's a little store in Milford that might have what you need—they'll definitely have the candles and incense, but I doubt they'll have a sword in stock. There are a few places on the Internet that would have everything on your list, but it might take a week or longer to get it all here."

"Too long," Douglas said, stiffening in alarm. He had no idea what Internet could be, but a week was out of the question.

"I know. I think our best move is to call a friend of mine. Michael will have everything we need. I would really like for him to meet you, Doug. Is it all right if I promise him that you'll show him some magic?"

Douglas couldn't keep his confusion off his face. "But if he's a wizard—"

Alex raised a hand. "He's Wiccan like me, but unlike me he does practice the craft. Michael leads the Silver Mist coven in Los Angeles. A few years ago, he tried to teach me how to control my gift, but it didn't work out. I know this all sounds strange, Doug, but what you showed me with the chair would mean a very great deal to him. Michael believes in magic—you won't have to prove to him that it exists—but the magic he knows is a subtle thing. Your little apprentice spell is big magic here."

Douglas nodded slowly. He should have expected something of the sort from Alex's reaction. His magic felt weaker than he was used to. How would it feel if he had never known any different? A simple levitation spell would seem amazing and powerful.

"I have no objections to demonstrating the spell for your friend."

Alex smiled in relief. "Thanks. It will mean a lot to him." Alex checked the kitchen clock. "He'll be at work right now. Why don't we go into town now and get you some fresh clothes. I can call Michael when we get back."

"I have to admit, fresh clothes sound very good to me."

"Come along, then," Alex said, reaching for her keys next to the sink.

* * *

9~Side Tracked

Tomas checked for outstanding warrants on one Douglas Skeldon as soon as he returned to his office. When nothing came up, he checked for warrants on anyone named Douglas or Doug. The few who came up didn't match Skeldon's description. One or both names could be an alias. He frowned at the computer and decided to look through the latest bulletins on the off chance a description would match Alex's new friend. He was barely half way through the list when Jenn stepped into his office.

Jenn closed the door and stood watching him. "What you doing, boss?"

"I was just out at Alex's place," he said glancing up from the computer screen. "She has a friend staying with her."

"Yeah?" she said, sounding surprised. "A man friend?"

"Yeah, so?"

"Nothing," Jenn said with a poker face.

Tomas wasn't buying. "Don't give me that! What does it matter if he's a guy or not?"

Jenn shrugged. "You tell me. You're the one who looks like a kid who lost his puppy, not me."

Tomas scowled.

"So, what are you doing, looking for a warrant to bust him with?"

Tomas quickly logged off. "Of course not."

Jenn chuckled. "You were! Hoowee, you've got it bad!"

"What we had ended a long time ago, Jenn. That has nothing to do with this. His name might or might not be Doug Skeldon, but they both lied about how they know each other. Alex said she met him on vacation last year. She gave me some bullshit about a road trip, but he's got a busted leg and her truck has a nice new dent in it. I'm guessing she hit him sometime over the last few days and is lying to protect him from me."

Jenn frowned worriedly. "Alex wouldn't do that."

Tomas just raised an eyebrow.

Jenn shrugged uncomfortably. "Okay, she would, but only if there was a damn good reason. You can't think he has anything to do with Sharon's murder."

"Maybe I can and maybe I can't," he said, but deep down he knew Alex would never cover for someone dangerous to others. She might not care for her own safety however. "At the moment I'm just scratching an itch. As soon as I learn something definite, I'll have some hard questions to ask both of them. At the very least, Skeldon is a stranger to these parts. That in itself is suspicious with what's going on around here."

"Okay, I can see that. Maybe Doc Williams knows something about him. Alex would have called him if she called anyone."

"Williams is next on my list." Tomas leaned back in his chair and clasped his hands behind his head. "How goes the search?"

Jenn's face turned disgruntled. "About the same. There are a hell of a lot of places for a man to hide around here. It will take time. I wish Alex could have been more specific."

"South," Tomas mused staring up at the ceiling. "She said

south of town. Okay, what's south?"

"There's the quarry."

"And the old cement works," Tomas agreed, looking back to Jenn as she took a seat. "Who have we got out there?"

"Ben took it."

"Okay. Ben's good. There's the old mill."

"Yeah, I thought of that, but it's more east than south."

Tomas frowned. "I don't like it that we're taking Alex's bullshit as gospel, Jenn."

"Come on! You know it's more than that."

"Maybe I do, but we're going all out to the south and ignoring other areas. Alex didn't say he was living south, she just said there was a shadow to the south."

"What else could it be?"

Tomas couldn't imagine what Alex saw in her head, and often thought she didn't understand half of it either. "I have no idea, but even if he was south that day, it doesn't mean he lives there, does it?"

Jenn frowned. "I guess not. You think she's holding out on us?"

Tomas shook his head. "Not about this. As for Skeldon, I'll talk to Williams before I decide what questions to ask. When you get right down to it, whether I trust Skeldon or not doesn't matter. As long as Alex won't come in, she needs someone out there, and she obviously does trust him. Busted leg or not, I'm thankful she's not alone."

Jenn nodded. "Makes sense. You still want Meeks keeping an eye on her?"

"Absolutely. He stays until this is over."

"Okay, I'll trade off with him. I don't want him falling asleep out there."

Boredom was always a problem when staking out someone's property. Until recently, Tomas had always put Alex's reluctance to sell the farm down to pure stubbornness, but that was before Sharon Brydon's murder. After seeing and feeling what he had when he touched her that night, he realised that Alex needed seclusion. It wasn't, and probably never had been, that she liked living alone; she *needed* to be alone just to function. That was a hard lesson for him to learn. It also raised the question of Skeldon's presence out there and how it affected Alex's condition.

"Keep it low profile, Jenn," Tomas said, thinking about the fuss Alex would make if she found out. "She almost bit my head off when I went over there and suggested she come in."

"I'm not surprised, and you should have known better."

"I did, I do know better, but seeing her out there with her nearest neighbours ten or twenty miles away…" He shook his head. "I had to try again."

"I'll make sure she doesn't see us."

Tomas stood and reached for his hat. "Good. I'm going to see Doc Williams. Hold the fort for me."

Tomas didn't have time to talk with Williams that day. He was driving to the hospital when his radio came to life asking him to return to the station. Sheriff Larson from Westwood had come for a visit. Tomas grumbled but made a u-turn and drove back. What the hell did Larson want? It was a long trip for a courtesy call, and if it was business, why not use the phone?

Larson rose from Tomas' visitor chair when he entered his office. He held his hat in one hand and a thick folder in the other. It was a business trip then. That relieved some of Tomas' tension. He was too damn busy for courtesy calls. Tomas shook Larson's hand and rounded his desk. He threw his own hat onto the filing cabinet as he sat.

"What can I do for you, Ian?" Tomas said, resting his forearms on the desk and leaning forward.

Ian Larson was new in his position. He had only been sheriff of Westwood since April when his predecessor retired after twenty years in the job. He had a tough act to follow. He was young for it, but as far as Tomas knew, qualified. Ten years experience was enough to learn the job, but whether that made him just competent or good at it remained to be seen. Not that Tomas had any say in the matter, but he did have to deal with Larson and others like him and it would be nice if Larson knew what he was doing.

Larson raised the folder in a sort of wave. "Got a case file here; wanted you to take a look before I asked for your help with it."

He didn't sound happy, Tomas mused. Couldn't blame him really. New in the job and already out of his depth, it must piss him off to ask for help from someone older and with more experience so soon.

"Okay," Tomas said reaching across the desk and taking the offered folder. "Let's take a look here."

Tomas opened the folder and went straight for the crime scene photos. Tomas froze as soon as he saw the victim's injuries, but he covered his reaction a second later by leaning all the way back in his swivel chair and crossing his legs. He balanced the folder on his raised knee, and started reading from the beginning. The victim was one Terrance Daniels, thirty-four years of age, white male found dead by his brother in his storage locker. The locker had been cleaned out of whatever it had contained, and the brother professed not to know what that had been. Riiight. It was amazing how many people thought cops were stupid.

Tomas continued his reading and the details went into his brain where he could recall them later, but his thoughts kept turning to the crime scene photos. It was obvious that the rune killer had visited Westwood. There was no doubt in his mind. Larson must suspect their cases were linked, why come here otherwise?

Did Larson expect to take over now?

Tomas wasn't comfortable with that idea, not unless it was certain the rune killer had relocated permanently. There was no way to know that until more bodies turned up in Westwood. One corpse wasn't enough to indicate a change in pattern, but it was suggestive. Alex's Shadowman had cleaned up after himself by killing Evan Currie and his driver, John Russell. Alex had even mentioned that killing the golden goose, meaning the drug dealing Currie, might mean he was getting ready to move on. Seems she might be right, again.

What did it all mean? Had his rune case gone south for the winter? Is that why Alex was sure the killer was south? Westwood was south, but that isn't what he thought Alex had meant. South of town, she had said. South of town meant south but *close* to town, at least it did to Jenn and him, but maybe it didn't to Alex. Tomas shook his head, dismissing the thought. It didn't really matter now. Larson's file indicated the rune killer had been in Westwood if he wasn't right this minute. That was what he needed to concentrate on. He tilted his chair upright and shuffled the pages back into order. He placed the folder neatly on his blotter and aligned it precisely with the edge of the desk.

"So, my rune killer has relocated... maybe," Tomas said.

Larson nodded. "I need everything you have on this case. I need to catch this fucker before the bodies start piling up in my town like they have here."

Tomas gritted his teeth angrily. That was a backhanded slap at him. Larson would regret that. "Hmmm, I'm not in the habit of giving files to just anyone. This is my case."

Larson's eyes narrowed. "You know this is the same guy."

"We don't know that for sure. It could be a copycat. Damn newspapers," Tomas said blandly.

"Don't be a fool, Edwards; you know this isn't any damn copycat. The runes are identical. That was never leaked to the news people."

Tomas shrugged.

Larson fumed.

Tomas didn't show his amusement or satisfaction, but he

felt it. Larson thought he could just come in and take over did he? He thought he could throw insults around and then walk away with his case files? Dream on.

Tomas drummed his fingers atop the file. "I suppose I could share the case," he said making his voice sound reluctant. "Westwood isn't really that far from here, maybe his territory is just bigger than we thought. We don't know where the next body will turn up. Could be here in Susanville for all we know, or even Leavitt. The Brydon girl came from there after all, and compared with the others she is the odd one out. We don't even know if he will kill again." He would, Tomas had no doubt of it, but there was no evidence to make that certain.

Larson grimaced, showing what he thought of that. "Joint jurisdiction is out of the question."

Tomas shook his head and waved that away. "Not joint jurisdiction. You're right about that. Totally out of the question, but I propose we work the current evidence together. I'll open my files to you. You do the same for me. I'll show you my scenes, and you show me yours."

"Who gets the credit when we catch him?" Larson said.

Tomas didn't sigh. Larson was new and had to make his mark. "Depends where he's caught I guess. If your guys run him down then it's yours. If mine do, it's mine."

Larson nodded slowly. "That's fair. Which of us leads the investigation?"

"I have three dead, you have one. I lead."

Larson shook his head. "I have the freshest scene and evidence. It has to be me."

Tomas actually agreed with him, but he didn't want to let Larson off that easily. He opened the file as if wanting to refresh his memory. Picked up a few pages, read a few paragraphs, and then closed the file.

"What do you think of the drug angle?" Tomas said. "You think Daniels was into the scene?"

"No, but he *was* known to us."

"For?" Tomas asked.

"Handling stolen goods, but most recently illegally modified weapons."

Tomas raised an eyebrow. "Guns?"

Larson nodded. "Machine guns and rifles mostly. Hand guns too, but it's the modified stuff that got him into trouble."

"Do you think it has any bearing on why he was killed?"

"Definitely. Deal gone bad is my favourite explanation right now."

Tomas grinned. "Yeah, nice and neat. You know about my dead dealer. I'm wondering if his product paid for your guy's guns, but why kill him?"

Larson shrugged. "Why kill the Brydon girl? What's the connection between her and the dealer, is there one? Your guess is as good as mine."

Unfortunately, that was true. Sharon Brydon's murder was the odd one out. It didn't fit the pattern they were seeing. She was the only female victim so far, the only one abducted and killed at a remote location, and she was the only one without a criminal record. In short, she didn't fit. All the other victims had criminal records. Ethan Currie and John Russell had known each other for years. They had "worked" together and even shared a jail cell once. Alex had connected them when she worked her mojo at the morgue as well, but although Russell had driven the car and helped abduct Sharon Brydon, there was no previous connection with the girl.

"The only connection we've uncovered is the car."

Larson grimaced. "No you haven't. Your pet psychic gave you that, and anything she says is inadmissible at best. At worst, it's total bullshit. A jury will laugh it out of court and you know it."

Tomas' eyes narrowed. "Alex Yorke is a resource. She has been invaluable."

"I know you two have history, but I'm not letting her get

any further into this. I don't believe in her brand of crazy, and I think you're mad to use her."

"She gave me the license plate and forensics confirms the car was used in Sharon Brydon's abduction. Explain that."

"I don't have to explain anything. She's out."

Tomas pursed his lips. "You can keep her out if you want, but if any more bodies turn up around here, I reserve the right to call her in. Not saying I will, but if I think I need to, then I will."

Larson shook his head. "That's between you and her, but you better not fuck up my evidence. I'm going to nail this guy."

"Sure," Tomas said. He couldn't blame Larson for his attitude. Not many would believe what Alex could do without witnessing it. "Sure you are."

* * *

10~Old Friends

A few days after meeting Douglas, Alex drove to Reno to collect Michael and his wife from the airport. To her relief, Michael had been delighted to hear from her. She had been a little worried about it, as they hadn't parted on the best of terms.

She checked her mirrors and changed lanes smoothly. "It's really good of them to come on such short notice, don't you think? I hope the plane is on time. I can't wait to see them again. You're really going to like Michael."

"He is a good friend?" Douglas asked, looking at the view through his window. A semi rumbled past and he turned to regard Alex. "A friend of your father perhaps?"

"Not of my father. My parents died when I was little, and I my grandparents raised me at the farm. Michael and I haven't seen each other for quite a while now, but he was a very good friend to me back then. I needed someone who understood what I was going through and he came closer than anyone ever has."

"How did you meet, then?"

She glanced at Douglas then back to the road when she found him watching her. "After graduation I moved to Los

Angeles—that's a big city to the south. Anyway, he used to come to circles at my friend's house once a week. I wasn't working with the police then. I was still studying for my degree. Both of us found the Goddess and the God while in college and became Wiccan around the same time—it gave us something in common to talk about. Michael was a very shy person then, but our shared belief in the Lord and Lady let him talk to me without him getting flustered. He was very sweet... I think he might have had a bit of a crush on me in the beginning, but he met Sandy not long after and that was that. Good thing too, it would have been awful trying to tell him I didn't feel that way about him." Alex smiled remembering her friends together. They were a great match. "Anyway, Michael was looking for something to belong to, and he found it when he joined Silver Mist. I was looking for answers about myself and my gift. He could see I was in some kind of trouble. My magic..." She grinned at Douglas. "I still can't get over that."

"You've known for years that you had power, Alex. I'm sure your friends tried to tell you what your gift meant."

Alex nodded, remembering the many circles where they had tried to explore her power. "They did, but I didn't believe them. That's part of the reason we haven't seen each other for so long. When Michael hears about all this, he's going to be impossible for weeks."

Douglas shook his head gently. "He will be happy for you, I should think."

"Sure he will. But he's going to gloat about it for days, and say *I told you so* about a million times! When he married Sandy, everyone was so surprised. We never thought he would come out of his shell, but he did. That was about two or three years ago now. I'm sure you'll like them."

"Alex?"

She glanced at him. "What?"

"There's no need to be nervous. I'm sure I'll like any friend of yours."

She sighed. "Right. Okay, you're right, I am nervous. It's just that we haven't seen each other for quite a while, and we didn't part on the best of terms. I just want you all to be friends."

"We will."

Alex nodded and concentrated on her driving.

They arrived at the airport in plenty of time. Michael's flight wasn't due until three, but she hadn't wanted to chance the traffic and possibly miss him. Thankfully, that hadn't happened and she spent the hour-long wait answering Douglas' questions about what he was seeing. The first time he saw a plane land, he was wide-eyed with amazement, especially when it taxied closer to the terminal and he could judge its size.

"What is that?"

Alex craned her neck. "A fuel truck. I'm pretty sure they put it in the wings of the plane… yes, there, see?"

Douglas nodded, watching the men hook up the fuel lines. "Fuel makes it go. What kind does it use?"

"A special gasoline I think; not like my truck."

"From oil again?"

"That's right," Alex said then made a face. "I'm sorry, but I don't know how a jet works. All I know is that the fuel makes the engines go, and they push the plane along very fast. When it gets going fast enough, the air passing over and under the wings lifts the plane into the sky."

Douglas shook his head gently in amazement. "And it can go anywhere in your world, even to lands across the sea?"

She nodded. "Anywhere there is a place to land like this. It might have to land for more fuel before continuing on. It depends how far away you want to go."

"Your people have much to be proud of, Alex."

Alex was pleased he thought so. "Americans *are* a proud people I guess. Our country is a young one, too."

"Yes?"

"A little over two hundred years."

"Two hundred…" Douglas shook his head in bemusement. "You have built all this in only two hundred years?"

"There were people here long before that, but America as a nation is only two hundred years old."

"Amazing. Perhaps this is the result of a people always in a hurry."

Alex grinned. "Maybe." She noted another plane taxiing toward the terminal and checked the time. "That's Michael's plane coming in now. Let's go meet him."

Alex was careful to walk slowly so that Douglas could keep up with her. She sometimes forgot that he was injured. He never complained, but she knew it must be frustrating for him. Doc said the cast should remain in place for at least three weeks and probably closer to six. Douglas had been grim and silent upon hearing that. She knew he had no intention of being laid up for that long. She could only hope his leg would be healed enough when his patience ran out.

Alex stationed herself at a point where Michael would be sure to see her, feeling a flutter of anxiety in her stomach. It was silly, but what if Michael was still angry with her? No, that couldn't be. He had sounded genuinely happy when they spoke on the phone. It would be all right. If she had anyone to worry about it was Sandy. They had been good friends at college, but their friendship had cooled when she married Michael. Alex had never felt for Michael what Sandy did, but she wasn't sure Sandy believed that. Things had felt strained between the three of them since the wedding. Not that Sandy was horrible to her or anything. Alex could be imagining it all, but something said she wasn't. She would never deliberately scan a friend, but sometimes she wished Sandy would let something slip into her public mind. At least then, she would know for sure if a problem really existed.

"Alex!"

She waved. "Michael!" He rushed forward. She was sure

he was going to hug her, but at the last moment, he seemed to remember her problem and stopped himself from touching her.

"It's great to see you!" he said as Sandy arrived at his shoulder, taking his arm possessively. "You look well. Doesn't she look well, Sandy?"

"Very well," Sandy said dryly and rolled her eyes at Alex.

Alex relaxed. There was no sign of the strain she remembered between them. Maybe she really had imagined it. Had it just been an excuse to leave? She wasn't sure now, it was too long ago, but it felt like old times again.

"This is Douglas Skeldon," she said, taking Doug's arm and saw surprise in their faces. They knew she couldn't casually touch people. "Doug, this is Michael and Sandy Norris."

"Honoured," Douglas said with a small bow.

Michael raised an eyebrow at the courtly display and shook Douglas' hand. "Pleased to meet you, Doug. I'm looking forward to the demonstration. Alex was very careful not to tell me what this is all about, but I wouldn't miss it for the world. Whatever she thinks is worth seeing must be something special."

Douglas smiled. "Special? That I don't know about, but Alex seemed quite excited by it."

Alex snorted. "Take no notice of him, Michael. I promise you, you'll be impressed."

Sandy nudged Michael, and he turned to look over his shoulder for a moment, before turning back to Alex. "I hope you don't mind, but I couldn't resist. I asked some of the others if they would like to come with us. I couldn't leave them at home after your tantalising offer."

Just then, four more people arrived to cluster around them. Mark and Susan were acquaintances from the past. Not good friends like Michael and Sandy, but at least Alex knew them. She had never met the other two. The man was skeletally thin and darkly tanned with sunken cheeks, but bright inquisitive eyes. He wore dark pants and a white shirt casually open at the collar revealing a little chest hair. He smiled at Alex in a friendly way, and she returned it. The woman wore a red shirt and matching jacket. The oldest among them, she had greying hair tightly held in a bun at the back, and had a pair of reading glasses hanging around her neck by a gold coloured chain. Her grey eyes looked hard. Alex had a feeling they didn't miss much. She reminded Alex of a stern professor who had taught psychology at college.

Michael made introductions while Alex frantically tried to fit this turn of events into their plans. More importantly, she had to fit them into her house!

"...you know they would have come if they could, but never mind. They told me to say they're thinking of you," Michael was saying, oblivious to Alex's worry. "Mark and Susan you know of course, but I don't think you ever met Alison Cully and Lloyd Hawkridge."

"No," Alex said, bracing herself before shaking their hands. When nothing happened, she released her breath in a silent sigh of gratitude. "When did you join Silver Mist?"

Lloyd answered for both of them. "About a year ago it was. I moved to Los Angeles for my work and met Alison there. She knew someone in Silver Mist, and invited me along to join a circle as a guest."

Alison glowered at Douglas; he returned it in full measure. Alex glanced at the two and hoped there wasn't a problem. She didn't know what was going on between them, but something obviously was. Michael and Sandy didn't seem aware of it, but Mark and Susan were. They were grinning at something. Douglas was bristling; he had drawn himself up to his full height to look down on Alison, and his arm felt rock hard with tension where Alex held it.

"Doug?"

"What?" He pulled his eyes reluctantly away from Alison. "Did I miss something? I'm sorry."

"No, you just seem preoccupied."

Alison snorted and Douglas gave her a wary glance before answering. "Preoccupied. That's one way of putting it."

"Is there a problem?" Michael asked, looking back and forth between the two. "Alison?"

"Not yet."

"Doug?"

Douglas shook his head. "No. No problem."

Michael frowned but then he shrugged. "Well in that case, I think we should fetch our luggage."

Sandy nodded, and after reading the notices nearby, she led the way.

"Michael, I don't know how to put this," Alex said, walking by his side. "But you should have asked me about bringing the others, or at least told me. I haven't room at the farm for all of you."

Michael waved that away. "Don't worry about that. We came prepared to find rooms in town."

"I had hoped… that is, I wanted you and Sandy to stay with us at the farm."

Michael's face fell; he was like a kicked puppy. "Oh, I'm sorry Alex. I should have thought. I'm sure the others won't mind if we split up. Sandy and I can—"

"No." Alex sighed. "That's all right. It wouldn't be fair on the others. It's fine, really."

Michael nodded. "If you're sure."

"I'm sure. Let's get your luggage and then sort out a rental car."

Michael joined Sandy as she watched for their luggage. Lloyd had already claimed his case and was helping Alison with hers. Alex fell back beside Douglas to watch. Michael found a trolley and deposited a huge trunk on it. Sandy added a pair of suitcases to the growing pile.

Alex glanced at Douglas then back to the others. "Are you sure you're okay?"

Douglas nodded. "Michael has power, and so does Alison. I felt nothing from the others, but they didn't try to cast their senses. I might have missed it."

"Cast their senses?"

"Alison used witch-sense on me. It was… I was a little surprised. I'm sorry if I seemed upset."

Witch-sense, what the hell is that? "I don't know what witch-sense is, Doug."

He frowned. "I don't know if I can explain it properly, Alex. Without training, a lot of it would make no sense to you."

"Try. Can you do it?"

"We—men I mean—have to cast a specific spell. We don't usually bother; the result isn't worth it. When a witch uses witch-sense on someone, it's like being questioned silently. It's more than that, much more, but I do not have the words. You have to experience it, Alex, to know how it feels."

The longer Alex hung around with Douglas the more she found she didn't understand. She had studied with Michael and others off and on for years, and she had never heard of such a thing.

"So, Alison asked you questions in your mind?" Alex wondered if it might be something like she did when listening to thoughts.

Douglas shook his head. "Nothing so courteous as that. Witch-sense does not *ask* for information, it *takes* it. The ungifted cannot stop it, and cannot hide anything from a witch using it."

Alex nodded. It sounded like something she had done before she set herself a few ground rules. She called it deep scanning; she never did it anymore for fear of what she would learn.

"What did she learn about you?"

Douglas' smile was a little smug. "Nothing. I can block the probing, but it's uncomfortable to do. In my land, using witch-sense on someone without permission is considered without honour."

"But it still happens, doesn't it?"

Douglas laughed. "All the time, Alex. Daughters of the Mother can be high handed, but to be fair, so can the Guild at times even though it's meant to prevent abuses of magic."

Why would Alison deep scan Douglas? Did it mean anything, or did Alison always do it when meeting someone for the first time? She shifted uneasily when she remembered this was her first meeting with Alison too.

"This is the first time I've met Lloyd and Alison," Alex said, watching Michael's friends chatting together. "They seem nice enough."

"I'm sure they are."

"What aren't you telling me?"

Douglas didn't look at her. He kept his eyes fixed on Alison. "Why do you think I'm hiding anything from you?"

"Well, aren't you?"

Douglas shrugged. "There is much I haven't told you about myself, about my world, about the situation at home. All kinds of things."

She gave him a dirty look. "What about Alison; what aren't you telling me about her?"

"I don't know the lady. What could I tell you that Michael cannot?"

"I don't know, but something."

Douglas smiled. "You have a lot of faith in my judgment."

Alex looked askance at that. "Yes I do."

Douglas' smile drained away. "Alison makes me uneasy. I don't know her, she's done nothing against me, but I don't trust her. She reminds me of other witches I've met in my time."

"In what way?"

"There are..." Douglas frowned. "I suppose you would call them factions. The Pact is not universally respected as it once was. There are witches that would like to see it dissolved, and the Guild with it. They don't trust men."

Alex grinned. "You think Alison is a man-hater?"

"Like those witches on my world, I think she would prefer all power in her hands, or at least in a woman's hands."

"But Michael leads her coven. He's a man."

Douglas shrugged.

As soon as Michael and the others had collected everything, they walked to the car rental place. Rather than rent two cars, they opted for an SUV big enough to carry all six of them and their luggage. Alex assumed the steamer trunk contained everyone's tools and Michael confirmed it later. He had brought everything she asked for and then some. Michael gleefully explained that he had enough stuff for a dozen demonstrations, and intended Douglas to use it all before they left for home.

Outside the airport, Alex helped Douglas into her truck and then turned back to Sandy. "Follow me into town. I'm sure there will be room at the hotel."

"Okeydokey," Sandy said and climbed behind the wheel of the SUV.

Alex pulled into traffic and watched in the rear view mirror as Sandy got on her tail. She drove in silence for a short while until they were on the main route back to Susanville. It was pretty much a straight run, and would take roughly an hour. As soon as she was sure Sandy was settled behind her, she relaxed.

"So, here we are," Alex said. "What did you think of Michael?"

"He loves his wife and you very much."

She swerved a little in surprise. "Me?"

"It is obvious."

"Really?"

Douglas nodded. "Sandy knows that about him."

"How do you know?"

"I asked her."

"You *what?!*" Alex yelped. She remembered them chatting together while she went with Michael to check out the SUV. "I thought you were just passing the time of day!"

"We were."

"Goddess, Doug! Where do you get off asking her something like that?"

Douglas shrugged. "She volunteered it. We were talking about you, and she told me about how you walked out on Silver Mist. Do all witches name their covens here?"

"Yes, and don't change the subject."

Douglas shrugged again. "I was only interested. It is something our worlds have in common. Sandy says Michael was very upset when you walked out on him."

Alex cringed. "I didn't walk out on him."

"Apparently he didn't see it that way. Sandy told me that he was ready to pass leadership of Silver Mist to one of the others and come after you."

Alex hunched her shoulders defensively. "Lord and Lady, I didn't know that." Michael had been so proud when the others asked him to lead the coven. For him to throw that over meant more than it might appear to outsiders. "Why didn't he come to see me?"

"Sandy told him why you had to go and persuaded him not to. It was a good thing you spoke with her before you left. Why did you?"

"Talk to her, you mean?"

Douglas shook his head. "Why did you leave?"

"You know why. It was getting to the point where I couldn't enter a room without hearing people in my head."

"And is now any better?"

"You know it isn't. If I have time to prepare I can shut them out for a while, but it doesn't last. You have no idea how happy it makes me that I can't hear you at all. Sandy was always quiet, in my head I mean. If she hadn't been, we wouldn't have been roommates for more than five minutes. Michael and the rest of Silver Mist are like most people—loud."

"So you ran away to your grandparents' farm."

She squirmed, feeling defensive. "It's mine now and I didn't run away. I left."

"No difference, is there?"

"There is actually!" she snarled. "Michael meant well, they all did, but they couldn't help me. They did try, they tried hard. I didn't want to leave. My work with the police was important to me, but I couldn't carry on as I was. As I am."

Douglas was quiet for a few seconds then said gently, "So you left all your friends, gave up and hid yourself away at the farm."

"That's right! I gave up. *Bad fucking me!* I thought at least you would understand. Just goes to show how stupid I am, huh?"

"But I do understand, Alex. I'm not judging you; I'm not in a position to judge anyone. Sandy told me what she thought your reasons were. I just wanted to hear it from you."

Alex's face heated. "Oh… sorry."

Douglas grinned. "It doesn't mean I agree with you."

She scowled, but then shook her head and laughed lightly. "Okay. So now you know all about me—"

"Hardly."

"—let's talk about you for a change."

"What would you like to know?"

"Everything."

Douglas chuckled. "Everything? Well you know my name is Douglas, and that I am Duke of Skeldon in the kingdom of Inari. You know I am a weak wizard, and that I was foolish enough to spy on Duke Wallace and get caught doing it. What else would you like to know?"

"Are you married?"

Douglas didn't answer right away, but after a few moments in which Alex had time to curse herself for being too curious for her own good, he answered in a subdued voice.

"I was. She died."

Alex bit her lip. "I'm so sorry. If you don't want to talk about it, I'll understand."

Douglas drew in a harsh breath. "It's all right. It's been almost six years since Anna died. What can I tell you of Anna? Her beauty was as bright as a summer's day, her wit as sharp as the finest sword, and I loved her desperately.

"My father and her father were companions in their youth. It had long been their wish to join our families. I was betrothed to Anna on her very first birthday. I was only five at the time and didn't really understand what all the fuss was about, but the moment I looked into her eyes, I knew we would be together. We were great friends as children, for which I am eternally grateful. Marriage would have been torture for both of us should we have taken a disliking to each other."

Alex shook her head. "That's unbelievable."

"Why?"

"You were engaged to be married at five!"

"Alliances between noble families are often sealed by marriage. I was very lucky in that Anna's father lived within a few days' hard ride. I might have been betrothed to some harridan from the far side of the kingdom. As it was, Anna and I spent a great deal of our time together, getting into mischief and worrying our mothers sick."

Alex grinned. "I can imagine you running them ragged."

Douglas chuckled. "I did, both of us did. I was twenty-one and Anna was sixteen when we married. Nine months later my son was born. We named him Alwyn after my father." His face darkened. "The birth was a hard one. The midwives said Anna would have no more children, but they were wrong. Years after Alwyn was born Anna fell pregnant again. I was sick with worry, but she made light of it. She was so happy. She wanted a little girl."

"What happened?"

"The babe came early and the birth went badly. I used my

magic to soothe the hurt, and had my men scour my lands for a wizard or witch to help her, but it was too late. I couldn't stop the bleeding."

"How old is your son?" she said quietly.

Douglas sniffed and rubbed his face roughly. "Oh… Alwyn is ten. A fine boy and a credit to our clan. I named our daughter Anna. She's six going on sixteen." He chuckled. "It's almost as if my Anna were reborn in her. She's as much of a handful as her mother was at her age."

Alex smiled wishing she could meet them. "Who is looking after them while you're here?"

"My brother," Douglas said flatly and Alex looked at him sharply. Douglas nodded at her look. "Edmund and I are not friends, but he loves the children. He would make for an excellent father should the right woman be found for him. As it is, he rules in my place and is father to my children. I have no fear for them while Edmund lives."

"What about your parents?"

"They passed into the summerlands not long after Anna. Edmund and the children are all my family now."

Alex sensed she would be wise to leave Douglas alone for a while. She was sad for Alwyn and little Anna, living with their uncle and not knowing the fate of their father. She hoped they knew how much Douglas loved them. It was little wonder that he was so impatient to return home.

She knew he was concerned about the spell they were to perform. He was more worried than he let on. Would it even work? It must. Without it, they would have to rely upon Tomas and his people to find Karel. Tomas would do his best, she had no doubt about that, but it would take time—time in which more people might die. No, the spell would work and Douglas would go home. The thought was not as comforting as it should have been.

Alex wondered, and not for the first time, whether it would be so bad if Douglas was trapped here with her. It was selfish, but the thought that he might stay was pleasant; more than pleasant. It was wonderful that she couldn't hear what he was thinking. She didn't have to guard against accidentally touching him, and she finally had someone to talk to who could talk back. Katy and the horses had been her only company for months. She was safe with Douglas. To be able to let down her defences and just be with someone was wonderful.

She shook her head when she realised just how self-centred she was being. She should be thinking of him not herself. America wasn't his home. Earth wasn't even his world! Of course he must go home. Alwyn and Anna needed him, and if she had understood all he had told her about Wallace and Inari, the people of Skeldon needed their Duke. Douglas had no choice; he had to leave. The thought almost made her cry out in pain. She didn't want to be alone!

* * *

"Here, let me," Douglas said, hefting one of the cases.

"But your leg," Michael protested.

"It will be fine."

"Okay, if you're sure." Michael took the other case, the heavier of the two, and pushed open the door to his room. Alex and Sandy exchanged a smirk and followed them inside. "On the bed is good, Doug, thanks."

Douglas put the case on the bed as instructed, and went to the window to look outside. There was a car parked in the street opposite the hotel. It looked like Tomas' car. It had writing on the side and lights on its roof, but he didn't recognise the driver. He let the drape fall back into position and turned back as Michael's friends trooped in.

"Everything okay? The rooms have everything you need?" Michael asked.

"Ours is fine," Mark answered and Susan nodded.

"No problems here." Lloyd shrugged. "I can't wait to get

started, actually. When can we see the demonstration you mentioned?"

"It's a little public here, Lloyd," Michael said dryly. "I thought we would wait until we get to Alex's place later tonight. Alison?"

Alison shrugged. "I agree with Lloyd. We should have gone straight to the farm."

"I didn't say that," Lloyd protested.

Alex shook her head. "There isn't room there for all of you, not unless some of you want to sleep in the stables."

Lloyd grinned. "I've slept in worse places. I wouldn't have minded."

"I would!" Susan said and Mark laughed.

"Alex?" Douglas beckoned to her. "Can I have a few minutes?"

"Sure. What's wrong?"

"Maybe nothing but…" Douglas twitched the drape aside and Alex's face darkened. "I think Tomas has taken matters in hand."

"Why, that sneaky—"

"He cares for you," Douglas interrupted. "He wants you to be safe."

"Yeah," Alex sighed sadly, making Douglas wonder at her reasons. "I should have known he wouldn't take no for an answer. This might be a problem."

"It doesn't have to be. This man—whoever he is—probably has orders to watch you. I doubt he has leave to interfere with what you do. As long as we make our magic out of his sight, nothing bad should come of his presence."

"Okay, but what about after? You said that you need Karel. We can't have Tomas following us to wherever he's hiding."

Douglas nodded and peered outside again. There were a number of ways to deal with the man, but he had to restrict his options to something non-permanent. He didn't want to kill him for following Tomas' orders. Where would be the honour in that?

"I'll think of something," Douglas said as he imagined scenarios in which he made the man follow him into an alley if he could find one nearby. The town's buildings were laid out damnably far apart. America didn't seem to like alleys if this town was any indication. Curse the luck. "There are spells of concealment, but it might be better simply to knock the man unconscious."

"We can't do that!" Alex squeaked and everyone turned to look at her. She lowered her voice. "Assaulting an officer is serious, Doug. We could get into so much trouble!"

"I'm already in trouble, Alex, but I wouldn't willingly leave you in such a position. I will use a spell."

Alex bit her lip and nodded.

"One more thing: I think we should tell the others what this is all about. There is danger. They have a right to know just what it is they're getting into."

Alex turned to look at Michael who was watching them suspiciously. "You're right. You'll have to demonstrate your magic, but not here."

Douglas waved her concern away. "Here or at the farm makes no difference."

"I would feel better if you did it at the farm."

"Then I will wait."

Alex nodded. "Thanks." She went to join Michael and the others hesitating only briefly before telling them the truth. "Michael, everyone, I have a little confession to make."

"Oooh goody!" Sandy clapped her hands together. "When's the happy day?"

Michael and the others laughed, all except Alison. She was watching Douglas, perhaps wondering what he found so interesting outside. He let the drape fall and hobbled back to join Alex.

"I…"

"Just begin at the beginning, Alex," Michael said. "It can't be that bad."

"It's not bad, but I'm not sure you will believe us." Alex turned to Sandy. "I didn't ask Michael to come visit me just to see a demonstration. I wanted his help with a spell that Douglas needs to cast to find somebody. About a week ago, we had a murder just outside of town. Tomas, that's our local sheriff, asked me to take a look at the body."

"How awful!" Susan said.

"It was awful," Alex agreed. "You know I've worked for the police before, but this time was a little different. Sharon Brydon was murdered in a ritualistic way to power a spell. I don't want to go into details. It was horrible enough seeing it without trying to describe it again. Suffice it to say, the man responsible needs to be stopped."

Michael frowned and turned to Douglas. "And you think I can help you find this man?"

Douglas shrugged. "His name is Karel. Alex believes you can help us, and I trust her judgment."

"What was the spell supposed to achieve?"

Alex took a deep breath and said in a rush, "Karel killed the girl to open a gate to another world and he succeeded."

Mark chuckled but it trailed off into silence when no one else laughed. "Oh come on! You're a scientist, Alex. You can't pretend to believe this Karel character really found a way to do that."

"I saw it, Mark. I do believe it."

Mark scowled. "Being Wiccan doesn't make me gullible. If anything, it makes me harder to fool, not less! In my line of work, I've seen some amazing things, but opening gates to other worlds is pure science fiction!"

"This would be fantasy fiction," Lloyd said and smirked at Mark's darkening colour.

"Whatever! Magic like that is impossible!"

Douglas shook his head. "Why do you insist that such magic is not possible? Alex has told me of your science magic.

Isn't it true that a scientist must test something to prove its validity?"

"That's true," Alex said quickly and Mark's scowl deepened. "Well, it is!"

"She's right, Mark," Susan pointed out. "You've said the same lots of times, don't deny it. How many times have you gone to investigate something you thought was probably a hoax?"

Mark shrugged uncomfortably. "Hundreds, I guess."

"Are you going to tell me that you faked those investigations? That you had already made up your mind before you got there?"

"Absolutely not!" Mark said hotly, making Douglas wonder who else had accused him of doing that, and when.

Susan smiled and patted his arm. "Well then, this is no different."

"Alex and I need your help," Douglas said before Mark could rally. "In exchange I'm willing to demonstrate certain things, but not here. The sheriff has posted a man outside to keep watch on Alex. It would be best if the rest of our discussion was held at the farm in private."

"No one is trying to fool you, Mark," Michael said consolingly. "Alex wouldn't do that, and neither would anyone else here. I have no idea what the truth is, but I'm willing to stay and find out. Are you?"

Mark glanced at his wife and she nodded. "Okay, I'll stick it out, but you should have told us before we got on the damn plane. I could have brought my instruments."

"He doesn't mean that kind of instrument," Alex whispered and Douglas shut his mouth, his question about musical instruments unasked. "If we're all agreed, I say we head out to my place and get started. Once you've seen what I've seen, you will understand."

11~Demonstrations

Alex watched as Mark and Michael discussed the slowly spinning chairs hanging in the air. Mark tugged on the leg of one of the chairs, and shook his head. Michael stepped around the other side of the chair, and between them they tried to pull it down without success.

Michael stepped back shaking his head. "He did it without preparation and…"

"Yes, but…"

"Oh come on, Mark!" Michael hissed. "It's right before your eyes, man!"

Mark sighed and glanced over his shoulder at Alex. He grinned at her and gave her the thumbs up before schooling his features and turning back to Michael.

"I'm not as easily convinced as you, Michael. I want to test every…"

Alex turned away grinning and trying not to laugh. Alison had staked out her own puzzle. On the coffee table there was a bowl of water in which could be seen the image of a man. Douglas said that while it looked like a scrying of Mardus, it was in fact just a party trick. He had simply conjured forth the image of Mardus and set it within the water. He wasn't very good at scrying with water, or so he said. His element was fire.

Lloyd poked a finger into the bowl and Alison scowled in annoyance. He pulled it out when it had no effect on the image, and licked the water off his finger. He frowned and murmured something to Alison who then dipped her finger and tasted the results.

"Hot."

"And salty," Lloyd agreed. "But he purified the bowl with salt so that's not too surprising."

"But he used cold water and this is hot."

Alex glanced at Douglas where he sat on the couch in brooding silence. He was staring at the television with Katy in cat heaven upon his lap. She didn't think he was really watching the show he had selected. After demonstrating a few small magics—his words—he took no further part in the arguments about how such things were achieved. She thought he found all this rather tedious; necessary perhaps, but tedious. He had quickly performed his tricks, and then retired from the scene quietly. Now he sat staring at the television stroking Katy with mechanical motions, seemingly unaware of anything but her fur under his hand.

Alex wandered into the kitchen and found Sandy helping Susan make sandwiches. "How's it going?"

"Oh hi," Sandy said. "Great."

Susan grinned. "Has my mighty scientist solved the mystery?"

Alex chuckled. "No, but he's determined."

All three looked at each other in silence for a moment and then laughed. Sandy said it perfectly earlier: the world suddenly felt brim-full of possibilities. That was exactly how Alex had felt after witnessing the trick Douglas performed for her.

Exactly.

Sandy piled the sandwiches on a plate and put it on the

table with the others. They had made quite a spread. Alex snatched one off the plate and gobbled it.

"So," Sandy said and dipped her knife into the butter. "Now that the boys are out of the way, are you going to tell us?"

Alex swallowed. "Tell you what?"

"How you met Douglas of course."

"I ran him down with my truck."

Susan laughed. "Way to go, Alex!"

Sandy sniggered. "She always gets her man. She breaks their legs so they can't get away, and then she ravishes 'em."

"It was an accident!" Alex protested, trying not to laugh.

"Of *course* it was!" Sandy said. "So it was you that busted his leg?"

Alex nodded ruefully. "Yeah, it was. I thought I'd killed him... Goddess it was awful. I'd had one of my turns that night. I saw something that I thought Tomas needed to know, so I jumped into my truck intending to tell him. I was driving like a lunatic..."

"As usual," Sandy said dryly.

"...came over the hill and there he was in the middle of the road. I tried to avoid him, but I couldn't. I found him in the bushes. I thought... I thought he was dead."

Sandy rubbed her back comfortingly. "Shush, shush... it's okay kiddo. He's fine isn't he?"

"Doc said he is."

"Well then, I'm sure he must be right. What you told us at the hotel—it's all true isn't it?"

Alex nodded.

"How does Douglas know Karel?"

"They come from the same... place."

Sandy exchanged glances with Susan and said, "Does that mean what I think it does?"

Alex pursed her lips. "What do you think it means?"

"That Douglas and Karel come from the same world...

not Earth?"

"That's right."

"Goddess," Sandy breathed then her eyes sharpened. "Why?"

"Why what?"

"Why did they come here?"

Alex shrugged. "Douglas came through by accident. I saw how it happened. Karel though, he came on purpose and it's not the first time he's been here. He must have brought others with him last time, because Mardus wasn't in the vision I saw, but Douglas recognised him in one of the photos Tomas brought. I don't know what Karel wants, but Douglas says whatever it is won't be good for his people. He says Karel works for Duke Wallace... what?"

Sandy was staring at her as if she was mad. "This just takes getting used to."

"You're telling me!" Alex said and then frowned. "Douglas is an important man in his country."

"Yes?"

"He's Duke of Skeldon. I don't pretend to understand everything he's told me, but from what I can gather, he's one of only five dukes in the kingdom of Inari. Each one is supposed to have equal standing, but in practice, it isn't like that. The king is also Duke of Harden, but he's just a boy. His mother is regent for him, but she sounds like a complete idiot."

Sandy leaned forward eagerly. "So Doug is a powerful man. Rich?"

Alex shrugged. "I guess."

"Married?"

Alex shook her head. "She died. He's got two kids and a brother though."

"Oh."

Alex looked askance at that. "Oh? What do you mean oh?"

"Just oh," Sandy said but then she sighed in exasperation.

"Come on Alex! It's obvious you feel more than just friendship for the guy. I've been watching you. You can't keep your eyes off him!"

Alex squirmed, shuffling her feet. "You're imagining things."

"Am I? I don't think so." Sandy finished what she was doing and dropped the knife and other things she had been using in the sink to wash later. "You look good together."

Alex shrugged uncomfortably and leaned back against the table. "He's only been here a few days, and he can't stay."

"But you want him to. Am I right?" Sandy asked quietly.

Alex nodded miserably.

"Maybe if you asked him…" Susan began but Sandy reached out to stop her.

"It's gotten worse, hasn't it? Your gift I mean."

Alex's laugh was more like a sob. "Curse more like. Douglas is the only person I can stand to be in the same room with for more than a few hours—I can even hear you now, Sandy."

Sandy stepped back a little. "You couldn't before."

Alex tried not to feel the stab of pain Sandy's retreat caused her. "I could a little, but you were always very quiet. I could ignore it, but not anymore. When I asked Michael to come here, I thought you two could stay at the farm with me—I was wrong. It's lucky there was room at the hotel isn't it?"

"Alex I'm—" Sandy began.

Lloyd chose that moment to enter the kitchen. "Is there anything to eat… what?" He stopped just inside the door when they all turned to stare at him. "I'm sorry, did I interrupt something?"

"No, you didn't interrupt," Alex said. "Of course there's something to eat. Look at all this." She waved a hand at the banquet laid out on her kitchen table. "Sandy has outdone herself. Help yourself."

Lloyd glanced sceptically at each of them in turn, but then he shrugged and joined them at the table. He took a plate and piled sandwiches and cake on it. "I'll take some for Alison too." He filled another plate.

Alex nodded. "Okay, good."

Sandy waited for Lloyd to leave. "Alex I'm really sorry if—"

"Let's take some of this in to Michael and the others." Alex reached for the plates.

"Don't be like that," Sandy pleaded. "I can't help it that your gift scares me. It weirds me out that you can hear what I'm thinking. I'm sorry, but it does. I can't do anything about that."

"I know." Alex piled sandwiches onto plates as quickly as she could reach them. "It's okay."

"It's not okay!"

"I'm going to eat this in the other room," Susan said holding up her half-eaten sandwich and making her escape.

Alex sighed and turned to her friend. "Okay or not, it doesn't matter, Sandy. I'm used to this kind of reaction from people; I'm resigned to it at least. I can't do anything about it. I can't change it. I wish I could."

"I know you can't change it, but it does matter. It matters if it hurts our friendship. Has it hurt our friendship?"

Alex shrugged.

"*Has it?*"

Her eyes burned with unshed tears. "What do you want me to say? Should I say it doesn't change how I feel? It does change how I feel and... and it just does. It does, and I don't know what to say or do about that, Sandy. It hurts when people think things about me that I know aren't true. And now you're thinking them too. You were the only friend I had that I could really talk to..."

"Had?" Sandy asked intently.

"...and—what?" Alex stuttered trying to hold back the wails of grief building in her chest.

"You said had. You said I was the only friend you had. *Are* we still friends?"

"Can we be?"

Sandy bit her lip. She reached to take Alex's hand, but then her hands fisted when she remembered what could happen if they touched. "I think we can, I think we *are!* Just don't listen to my thoughts. Just don't listen all right?"

Alex hugged herself tightly. "It doesn't work like that, you know that."

"Can't you just lie to me for once?!" Sandy cried. "Just lie and say you won't listen."

"But..." Alex said feeling bewildered. Sandy's thoughts were in chaos. She couldn't get anything coherent from her. "I promise not to listen to your thoughts. Is that okay?"

"Yes!" Sandy snapped, but then she laughed. She grabbed Alex without thinking and hugged her hard. She didn't seem to notice the jolt like an electric shock that went through Alex's body at the contact.

Alex tentatively put her arms around her friend, all the while trying frantically to live up to the promise she had just made.

...thank the goddess for that... I love you, Alex. I always have. If I had a sister, I'd want her to be you. How I've missed you... can she hear me? Goddess I hope not. Think nice things just in case...

Alex grinned through her tears and finally managed to block out Sandy's thoughts. Think nice things. Sandy couldn't have thought of anything better to say than saying she loved her like a sister.

Sandy finally pulled away when she realised what she was doing. "I forgot. I shouldn't have touched you. I'm sorry."

Alex waved that away.

"Look at us," Sandy said wiping away her tears. "We're like a couple of kids balling their eyes out over nothing."

"Not nothing. You mean a lot to me—a lot. You and Michael are the closest thing to family I have… sister mine."

Sandy's eyes widened, but she didn't pull away. "We should take some food in for Michael and the others."

Alex nodded and began piling sandwiches on a second plate. She followed Sandy to the door carrying the food, but before they joined the others, Sandy said one thing more.

"Sisters. I like that."

* * *

12~Circle and Stone

Douglas took a sip of his coffee and frowned at its bitterness. He doubted he would ever come to savour the strange brew as much as the others so obviously did. Sitting opposite him, Michael chatted excitedly with Alex, who smiled and nodded at what he was saying. Lloyd sat this side of the table with Douglas, his elbows on the table and his cup cradled in both hands as he concentrated on his coffee to the exclusion of everything, while Susan and Sandy were talking about something they had both seen on Alex's *television*. That left Mark and Alison.

Mark had already finished his coffee, and busily scribbled notes on a notepad, his hand speeding across the page as if in a race with his thoughts. He was a freelance journalist. That was something like a scholar apparently. He spent all his time investigating strange happenings and news stories for a magazine that specialised in the weird—Alex's words. Mark's father was a senator. A powerful man that Douglas assumed was like unto a Duke in Inari. His father's money allowed Mark to pursue his studies to his heart's content. A somewhat frivolous life for a noble, but America was strange in many ways.

Alison stared silently at Douglas making him uncomfortable—something she seemed to take great delight in doing. There was something unnerving in a woman staring at him like that. It wasn't that she was a witch. Alex was a witch too, and he didn't mind her staring at him. Not that she ever had. Alex was a lady and too polite to do that. No, it wasn't that Alison was a witch that made him uncomfortable, or her use of witch sense on him at the airport. It was more her silences and considering looks that set his teeth on edge. If she had been a man, he would have been readying himself for a fight, for he would have assumed that Alison had some kind of quarrel with him demanding satisfaction in a duel. That was ridiculous here of course.

America was a land of laws and courts, not one of trial by combat as Inari sometimes seemed to be. Inari had courts too, but it was almost ridiculously easy to circumvent such justice. With witnesses on hand and according to custom, he could simply pick a fight and challenge his enemy to a duel. The survivor of such a challenge was deemed to be in the right, or innocent if the cause of the duel had been a criminal matter. Only merchants and commoners truly relied upon the courts. Even they would sometimes resort to the challenge circle. He knew of a few so-called merchant princes that were uncommonly good with a blade.

Swords and duels reminded him of his own lack of a good blade. "Michael?"

"Yes?"

"Are you satisfied that I'm no charlatan?"

"We never called you that!" Sandy protested.

"I did," Alex said and then grinned. "Well, as good as. I didn't believe a word he said until he made my chair float to the ceiling with me on it!"

Everyone grinned and chuckled at the image, all except Alison who was now sipping her almost cold coffee.

"If we're all agreed that I've told you the truth," Douglas

went on. "I'd like to talk about how we can find Karel."

Michael nodded. "Go on."

"I asked Alex to get me a few things so that I might use magic to find Mardus. If I can locate him, I'm sure Karel won't be far away. Even if Mardus is alone, I can make him tell me where Karel is."

"Makes sense," Michael said. He rose to his feet and crossed the room to the trunk containing his tools. "Alex asked me to fetch you a sword. I must admit that I was surprised when she asked for this—not many people use them as athames."

Douglas went to join Michael and took the weapon from him. It was a longsword with a simple brass pommel and cross-guard. He unsheathed the sword and made a pass with it through the air. It was a very fine weapon—well balanced and light, yet obviously strong. The blade itself was over a yard long and patterned over its entire length in ladder-like waves—an indication of a very fine weapon. Only the master swordsmiths knew the how of it, but all knew what it meant. This was a king among swords.

"This is too much," Douglas said regretfully. He offered the sword back to Michael. "It is too fine for me."

"It belonged to my father," Michael said, not taking it back.

"Even more reason not to take it then."

"You misunderstand me, Doug. My father was a bit of a war buff... I mean he collected memorabilia like old guns and swords. I have loads of his stuff back at my place. The sword is battle ready."

Douglas frowned. Battle ready? A sword that wasn't battle ready would be useless. "I don't understand."

"I mean it's not a replica. It's a real sword—very old. I don't know what he paid for it, but my mother was angry with him for a long time. It was relegated to a cupboard out of her sight. I know it would please him to know a real swordsman was carrying it again."

"I'm no master of the sword to be worthy of such a blade, but…" Douglas pressed the hilt of the sword to his forehead a moment. "I vow that no stain of dishonour shall mar it."

"Ermmm… okay," Michael said awkwardly. He shook his head a little and then turned back to the trunk. "I have a belt that came with the sheath in here somewhere as well as all the other stuff Alex wanted. Give me a hand; we can use the kitchen for the circle."

Douglas sheathed the weapon and helped Michael carry the supplies into the kitchen where the others joined them to watch. He laid his sword on a chair and investigated the items that Michael put on the table. Alex found the photograph of Mardus and put that on the table next to the other things. Michael withdrew four silver bowls from the trunk. They were engraved with runes of the elements, but they didn't look quite right.

Douglas frowned at them not sure he liked the differences. Errors in things like runes could have unintended effects. He wondered uneasily what other errors might come to light. He picked up each of the bowls and examined them critically trying to decide what the differences might mean to the spell. The runes of fire and wind looked quite similar to those he had used before. He decided that they would do. That left earth and water. Both were readily identifiable, but the engraving seemed overly ostentatious with many unneeded curves and extra lines. He went through the spell in his head again, but could not see how it would hurt to use them. The bowls had no part in the binding spell. He needed them only for the protective circle.

He would use them.

Douglas went through Michael's supplies discarding what he didn't need and piling useful items beside the bowls. When he finished, Michael put away the unwanted things in the trunk and sat with the others at the table to watch. There was plenty of space in the kitchen for the circle. There was no need to move the table out of the room.

Douglas pushed the trunk more into the centre of his chosen area and Alex draped a cloth over it. This was to be their altar. He placed the photograph of Mardus on the altar, and Alex added the map, a pair of candles, some amber for strength, amethyst to increase awareness, malachite for protection from danger, and a fragment of obsidian that he would use to help clear his mind ready to cast the spell.

Douglas turned to Alex. "You remember all I told you of the spell?"

Alex nodded and shook her box of matches. "I remember."

He nodded and turned back to the others. "No one is to talk. No one is to interfere. No matter what you think you see or feel, do not touch me or Alex until I break the circle. You aren't needed for the spell—should not really be present, but I don't think it hurts anything if you simply watch and take no part... I don't think it does. Under no circumstances try to leave the protection of the circle."

Michael answered for all of them. "We understand."

"I hope so. Karel is dangerous. If he should learn of what I do, he might try to reach me. I know how to protect myself from him. You do not." Douglas took up his sword and unsheathed it. "Has this ever drawn blood?"

"I'm sure it has," Michael said. "But I purified and consecrated it to the goddess when I knew I would give it to you."

"Thank you." He always purified his sword before working magic. "That simplifies matters greatly. Alex, the candles please."

Alex lit a few scented candles that she placed around the room. The kitchen was suddenly filled with the subtle scent of jasmine. While Alex busied herself with the candles, Douglas filled each of the four bowls with the things he had chosen to represent the elements. In the bowl engraved with the rune of air, he placed three black feathers to represent that element and the three incarnations of the mother. On top of the three, he placed one white feather to honour the god her consort.

"Why black? They should be white surely..." Sandy whispered. Douglas glared and that silenced her. "Sorry."

Michael and Sandy exchanged uneasy looks. Douglas was aware of a subtle tension beginning to build within the room. Alex's friends did not seem happy with his preparations. Perhaps they knew of another way in which the spell might be wrought. At some other time, he might have enquired, but not this night. He knew of only one way and would not complicate matters by experimenting.

He chose the bowl engraved with the rune of water. Alex handed him a bottle she had filled earlier with water from her spring. He filled the bowl. Again, his choice caused consternation among Alex's friends, but this time it was Michael who shushed the others. Douglas frowned hard at Alison. Her protest had been the first and loudest this time. He put all his worry and anger into the look. One more interruption, it promised, and he would insist they all leave.

He turned back to his work. Earth was next. He filled the silver bowl with salt to represent the element, and for fire he used a little molten wax to glue a short red candle into the bottom of the bowl. He placed all four bowls with his sword on the altar.

Michael and the others watched and their faces grew eager as he, holding the bowl of feathers high, began a chant while walking widdershins (counter-clockwise) around the room in a wide circle that encompassed the altar, the table, and everyone within the room.

"By the blessed breath of the goddess,
By winds blown cold and breezes fair,
Be cleansed of all evil and taint.
As I will, so let it be."

He stopped and placed the silver bowl upon the floor to protect the eastern quadrant of the circle. He moved back to the altar and took up the bowl with its red candle representing fire. Moving to the southern quadrant, he raised the bowl high in salute and walked the circle again chanting loudly.

> "By Her burning soul's desire,
> Dancing flames and burning fire,
> Be cleansed of all evil and taint.
> As I will, so let it be."

He placed the bowl on the floor to protect the south. The moment the bowl touched the floor, the candle took light and Douglas breathed a silent thank you to the goddess. He hadn't realised until that moment how much he had feared failure, but so far nothing was different. He felt at peace, as it should be, and the candle had lit, also as it should. Everything was fine. He took up the bowl of water and moved to the western quadrant of the circle where he raised it above his head in salute to the goddess. For the third time, he circled the room this time sprinkling a few drops of water from the bowl. He could feel the power of the circle beginning to stir like an invisible trail he left behind him.

> "By water that flows through Her veins,
> The force of storms and gentle rains,
> Be cleansed of all evil and taint.
> As I will, so let it be."

He placed the bowl upon the floor in the west, and took up the last bowl from the altar. Beginning in the north, he raised the bowl of salt in salute and then circled the room one final time. As he walked and chanted, he sprinkled some of the salt from the bowl.

> "By the Earth that is Her body,

By mountain, valley, hill, and mound,
Be cleansed of all evil and taint.
As I will, so let it be."

He placed the bowl upon the floor to protect the northern quadrant and returned to the altar. Raising his hands high, he tried to visualise moonlight filling the circle and cleansing it. It would have been far easier had he drawn the circle outside under the night sky, but Tomas had ensured he could not do that by leaving one of his men on watch at Alex's gate. She did not want to risk performing the ritual outside, not even out of Meeks' sight behind the house, in case Tomas should come by to check on her. The farm was big enough to hide them all easily, but that would make things worse. Tomas might send out search parties!

"A holy place, A circle round,
These elements of sky and ground.
By Air, Fire, Water, Soil,
Secure against corruption's toil."

He nodded to Alex. She stood and moved to the east quadrant. They had agreed earlier that she would call the quarters to protect the circle. It would be all the stronger for the true owner of the land and hearth to ask the protection of the elements.

"Come to us now, O winds of the East,
Whirl and twirl 'til the magic has ceased.
Blow through our hearts, and the energy raise.
Blow away clouds and blow away haze,
The circle is open—your power please lend,
Your presence is welcomed—we bid you come in!"

Douglas watched as Alex moved unselfconsciously to each quadrant of the circle in turn to invite the watchtower guardians to take their place in the circle. She performed the ritual flawlessly, though she had insisted she was unpractised in its use. She finished by inviting the element of earth to protect the north. When she was done, Alex returned to the altar to wait for him.

Taking up his sword, he moved to stand before the guardian of the east. He reached out to his taufr with his mind and drew power into the sword. Holding the hilt in both hands before his chest, he held the sword pointed down at the bowl for a few breaths before walking the circle—deosil (clockwise) this time. When he reached one of the bowls, he held the sword above it for a few breaths allowing magic to flow through his taufr into the sword and then into the bowl. He felt the flow of power fill each bowl, but there was nothing to see visually. He frowned when he realised that. There should be something… a light or a glow, but something. As he walked the circle, he frantically tried to think of something he had forgotten to do, but he had done this hundreds of times. He knew the rituals by heart. He hadn't forgotten anything; it was simply that the magic was weaker here.

He returned to the eastern quadrant, knowing that the circle was weak but not knowing what to do about it. He glanced worriedly at Alex, but she didn't notice. She was watching him full of trust unaware of the danger he would put her through if he cast the spell within a weak circle of protection. He couldn't risk it.

Not knowing what else to do, he began a second circuit and added a chant he had learned that might strengthen the circle's protection. He had never performed it before—he had never needed it. He walked the circle and tried to force it to manifest itself as a wall of light. He wanted the magic of the guardians to flow and link together as he had so often seen back home. He wanted it desperately.

"I cast you now, O circle of power,

I conjure your magic to grow and tower,
Dividing the world of ancients and mundanity,
The space where all magic lives and breathes,
Where time and place and mundanity cease,
Between the worlds, the circle is cast—
Meeting as one with present, future, and past.
The old ones and young ones join the night and the day,
And all that's mundane is now swept away.
All merry meet, suspended in time.
The circle is bound, by the words of this rhyme!"

There came a surge of power through his taufr and a pale glow sprang up around the circle. It was dim, barely there at all, but it gave him hope that he was on the right track. He decided to walk the circle a third time. The number three was sacred to the goddess. He hoped it would make all the difference. Alex was looking around at the palely shimmering wall of light in wide-eyed awe. If she had known how pitifully weak it was, she wouldn't be awed. She would be scared.

Douglas finished his third circuit and felt the circle's protection strengthen a little more. It might be strong enough to stop Karel from sensing anything. Might be. He wasn't confident and knew he would be in serious jeopardy despite the circle if Karel found out what he was doing. He had no choice but to finish what he had begun and trust in the goddess.

He lowered himself awkwardly to the floor opposite Alex with the altar between them. Alex lit the candles where they stood upon the altar and invoked the goddess and the god. Douglas thought it best he not interfere in this. They were in Alex's home and not his. This wasn't even his world! As he listened to Alex's prayer, he marvelled at the similarities and differences in it and wondered how such a thing had come to be.

He put aside his sword, withdrew his taufr, and placed it upon the image of Mardus. He arranged some pieces of amber, amethyst, and malachite around the picture and more around the map saving only the obsidian arrowhead. He planned to make the obsidian into a lodestone with Mardus as its north. If all worked well, it would be drawn to him. He placed the arrowhead on the map.

"Are you ready?" he said and Alex nodded. He took her hands over the altar. They were shaking. "Try to relax and remember what I told you. Don't resist me. It will hurt worse if you do that. All right?"

"I'm not afraid," Alex said bravely.

The trust he saw in her eyes made his guilt worse. He wanted to stop right now before he tested their friendship, before the trust in her eyes turned to hurt and accusation, but he couldn't. The spell had to be cast no matter what it cost him or Alex. Many more than two lives depended upon his return to Inari.

With his eyes fixed firmly upon Mardus' photograph, he took a deep breath and reached for Alex's magic. She felt the violation of her spirit instantly—felt him attempt to steal the power that was her birthright the instant he reached for it. Her eyes flew wide in shock. It hurt. He knew from experience that it did hurt, but it had to be done. The hurt was a small one compared to what Karel would inflict if he should escape.

"Relax Alex, don't fight me. Don't fight me!"

Alex gasped, "It…" **hurts!**

"I know, but don't fight me. Let me take it, let me use it… that's it. Relax, Alex. It will be over very soon. Just give it to me."

Douglas tried to be gentle, but no matter how much Alex said she hated her magic, it was part of her. She couldn't, even after all she had said, surrender it without a struggle even though she wanted to. He ripped it from her, knowing he hurt her but unable to do otherwise. Turning his thoughts of self-loathing at what he was doing into hatred of Mardus wasn't hard at all. It was Karel and Mardus' fault he needed to do this.

He sent Alex's magic seeking someone from Inari, someone not native to this world… someone like Mardus.

"What's happening?"

Douglas heard her as he heard his own thoughts. They were one until this was over. He felt her pain and tried to stand between it and her, but knew before he tried it wouldn't work. She was weakening as her magic flowed into him. He grew stronger as she grew weaker. He knew a witch could die of this draining. Alex would die of it were he of Karel's ilk. Draining a person this way was a foul use of power, as bad if not worse than blood magic. It was a dishonourable thing to do to anyone. It was rape, no other word sufficed. The stain upon his honour made him feel sick.

"It will be all right, Alex. Please trust me, just trust in me, please. Follow where the magic leads you. I am with you. Let us see what it finds."

Together they raced across the land. They sped over empty roads and country, passing people in their cars, racing down streets in the towns, plunging through walls and buildings without slowing. Time seemed suspended as they raced toward something that even Douglas did not know. He hoped, but he did not know. If Karel felt their approach, then it would be him and not Mardus they would find waiting for them. He tried to prepare himself for a fight, and prayed to the goddess that Karel did not learn of their approach.

Finally, the magic slowed in its search and tentatively approached a window. It flowed through into a room and waited. Douglas could almost feel its satisfaction at a job well done. It was most peculiar the way Alex's magic reacted to things. It was as if her magic was alive and not simply power to be used. Very strange indeed.

"That's him. Mardus," Alex said.

"Where are we?" Douglas said.

"Somewhere in Westwood I think. I recognised a few

things on the way."

"Westwood is the town in the photograph?" Douglas asked, wondering why Karel had chosen it, and if there was something he should worry over. Could there be a circle of power there?

"No, but Jenn told me that Karel did kill a man here. Another criminal she said. Why, what's wrong?"

"Nothing is wrong, Alex. It just seems strange that he stayed here. I would have expected him to move on."

"Why?" Alex said. "No one knows him. Only we know that he's involved in this."

"You're right. We should not linger here. Let me just touch him with your magic so that I might pass on the memory of his foul essence to the lodestone."

Douglas took a moment to look around hoping to divine Mardus' purpose for being here. The room was nothing special, just a room. Mardus was sitting on the bed sharpening a dagger while in the background the television was on filling the room with sound. Mardus wasn't watching it; he was too intent upon his weapons. Douglas saw a pair of daggers and a sword on the bed, but there were no guns. It surprised but pleased him that Mardus had not taken up the use of guns. He hoped Karel had not thought of it either. He reached out to touch Mardus with Alex's magic, and it was done. The moment past with Mardus continuing about his business unaware that anything had changed.

"We go back now, Alex. Quickly, lest Karel be near and sense us."

As quick as thought, they raced back to their bodies. Little time had past since they began, perhaps only a few breaths. It was difficult for Douglas to tell. When travelling out of body, time seemed suspended. It wasn't, but it did seem that way. That was one reason why journeying like this was dangerous. Staying away too long could weaken the connection between the spirit at its rightful house within flesh.

As soon as they returned, Douglas let his control of Alex's magic go. It snapped back into her giving him a nasty jolt as it did so by way of retribution. It was uncanny. It almost seemed that her magic had reprimanded him for trying to steal it.

Most peculiar.

Alex opened her eyes and winced at a blinding headache behind her eyes. Douglas knew how that felt. His head felt like it was going to split apart. Trying to distract himself, he turned his attention to the obsidian fragment and imbued it with the essence he stole from Mardus. He licked his finger, drew a rune of binding upon the fragment, and spoke its name. To be certain, he breathed upon it and sounded the binding again, and a third time.

> "Thrice I bind you, Mardus,
> See the sight, hear the sound.
> Thrice I bind you, Mardus,
> What was lost, now is found.
> Thrice I bind you, Mardus,
> Bound and binding, soul to stone,
> One to the other, until we be *home!*"

The spell settled into the stone and he breathed easier. There was nothing to suggest it was anything other than an obsidian arrowhead, at least not visually. It looked the same. The spell wasn't a flashy thing of lights and sound as sometimes was the case with rune magic, but there was no doubt in his mind that the spell was working. If he closed his eyes, it felt as if Mardus was right there in the circle with him. Very unsettling.

"Do you feel it?" Douglas whispered.

Alex nodded worriedly. "The stone feels like *him*— Mardus."

Douglas licked his lips. "I've never used the spell exactly this way before. I think that's normal. I think it's supposed to happen… I hope it is."

"Let me thank the goddess and dismiss the guardians," Alex said and climbed to her feet.

Douglas nodded his thanks. He was feeling a little out of sorts—shaky with a profound feeling of relief. The spell had worked! Despite all the strangeness of this world, despite the weakness of his magic, it had worked! He knew he had Alex to thank for this chance of getting home. He owed her a great debt. Not only had she cared for him after the accident, but now she had suffered pain and the violation of her spirit to enable him to go home.

The guilt he felt for what he had put her through made him almost physically ill. If told before this that he would be capable of violating a woman in such a manner, he would have reacted with outrage. Without hesitation, he would have sworn any oath that he was not capable of such a thing, but now he knew otherwise. The knowledge of what he had done to Alex was a heavy burden. He should have tried harder to explain what he planned to do before casting the spell, but his fear that she might refuse had made him downplay it. He would make it up to her somehow. Perhaps he could make a warding stone for her. It might help to bolster her shields. As she had no hope of proper training, she would need one or something like it.

Douglas watched her perform the ritual noting how practiced she seemed. Alex had told him that she had studied what she called the craft, but that she wasn't a practitioner of it. If not for her clothes and the surroundings, he could easily have believed her a witch from his own world. She thanked the goddess and the god for their presence, and invited them to stay or go as they willed before thanking the guardians and releasing them. She broke the circle with a simple rhyme.

"…Merry we meet, and now merry we part,
until we meet again with joy in our hearts."

Douglas felt the release of energy as the circle opened. Excited chatter filled the room as Michael and the others came forward asking Alex questions about what she had seen and felt. He struggled to get to his feet. Lloyd noticed and came forward to help. A chill gripped him when Alison picked up the arrowhead. He stepped forward with his hand out to take it, but she ignored him.

"The stone, please," Douglas said. "Give it to me, *please*."

"Alison?" Lloyd said in puzzlement. "Give him the stone."

"*Please*, I must have the stone," he said a little less calmly this time.

Alison smiled and then shrugged. She tossed the stone to him as if it were nothing to her. "No reason to get upset."

He frowned at the lodestone trying to detect anything amiss, but there was nothing. "Forgive me, but this is my salvation—a way home for me."

"Of course I forgive you," Alison said with a superior seeming smile.

* * *

13~Deceptions

Alex watched Lloyd weigh the lodestone in his hand.

He shook his head. "It's just another rock to me." He bounced the stone arrowhead on his palm and then past it to Susan.

"Same here," she said. "Nothing."

"May I?" Michael said and took the stone. "I feel something. Not sure what it is, but something. It's almost as if…"

"What?" Douglas said with a small smile.

"You'll think I'm crazy, but it feels like it wants me to take it to its master," Michael said looking embarrassed.

Douglas smiled. "You're not crazy. The spell we used is very like the spell of true ownership."

Alex frowned. "True ownership?"

Douglas nodded. "The true ownership spell is a far more powerful spell than I can do, but it's similar to my location spell in one of its effects. If I had really cast the true ownership spell on the stone, it would find its way to its owner—Mardus in this case—no matter how long it took or who it had to use to get there. It would literally force Michael to take it to Mardus. It might make him send it directly in some manner, or take it personally, or maybe even give it to someone else—someone more likely to reach its owner quicker."

Michael dropped the arrowhead onto the kitchen table and wiped his hand on his pants in distaste. "A compulsion then, but your spell is different you say. How?"

"Less powerful and much less complex. The location spell does have influence, but it exerts it over you in a different manner. It knows where it wants to go and lets you know too, but it cannot force you to take it there. All we have to do is heed it, and let it show us to Mardus. It's like a lodestone now. Mardus is its north."

Mark picked up the stone from the kitchen table and shook his head. "I can't feel anything either." He passed it back to Douglas. "So, what now?"

Alex had been thinking about that. "We have to fix officer Meeks somehow."

"Fix him?" Michael asked uncertainly. "Fix him how?"

Douglas shrugged. "I wanted to knock him unconscious, but Alex won't let me."

"I should think not!" Michael said, horrified by the idea. "He's a police officer. We would get into serious trouble!"

Douglas shook his head. "You don't know what trouble is, Michael. Meeks is nothing compared to Mardus and Karel, but I did promise Alex that I wouldn't hurt Meeks."

Alex shifted uncomfortably on her chair. "I could make him think Michael was Douglas and Sandy was me."

Michael opened his mouth as if to scold her. Influencing someone's mind with magic went against the Wiccan Rede, and it was just plain rude besides, but he hesitated. Alex knew what he was thinking: Mardus was a murderer; where in this situation was the more harm to be found—action or inaction?

Michael glanced at the others and made his decision. "It would be easier to make him think Susan was you, Alex. She's closer to your build, and Mark is about the same height as Douglas. I'm at least a foot taller than he is."

Alex covered her surprise at his easy acceptance of her idea. She nodded and looked at Douglas. "When?"

"Now," Douglas said instantly. "I don't know if Karel sensed us. I hope he didn't but I have no way of knowing for sure. If he goes back to Inari before I get to him…"

"You'll be stuck here," Alex said quietly.

Douglas nodded. "It has to be tonight. How long to get to Westwood?"

"Two hours or so."

"Perfect. I can take Mardus while he sleeps. That gives us all night to make him talk."

"Make him talk?" Lloyd said uneasily. "Make him talk how?"

Douglas smiled grimly. "Don't worry about it; I'll take care of it."

The silence was an uneasy one. Lloyd looked worried. Alison on the other hand, seemed almost eager to get on with it. Mark and Susan looked relieved to be left behind and Alex didn't blame them. Michael was frowning at the stone in Douglas' hand perhaps wondering about the right and wrong of the situation. Sandy's face was the only one she couldn't read. Whatever Sandy was thinking, it would take her gift to discover, and she had promised not to do that. It didn't matter. None of them were willing to back out now.

"…Alex?" Douglas was saying.

Alex shook off her preoccupation. "Hmmm?"

"Do you need to prepare? Is there anything you need?"

"Oh, Meeks… right. No. I mean no, I don't need anything, but I think we should get all our stuff together first. We can load up the SUV. It won't matter if Meeks sees that, he'll think Michael and the others are getting ready to go back to the hotel."

"Anything else?" Michael said.

She considered the problem. Making Meeks see what wasn't there could be done, but not easily. It would be better to give him something he expected, and then twist his perception of it. "If Mark and Susan could dress like us, it would make things easier."

Mark nodded. "We're about the same size. Let's switch clothes now."

Mark followed Douglas into his bedroom to change, and Alex led Susan into her room to do the same.

Alex stripped and held out her jeans and cardigan to Susan. She received Susan's skirt and blouse in exchange. As they dressed, Susan chatted about how exciting all this was. Alex just nodded or smiled in the appropriate places. She was thinking about Douglas leaving. If all went well, by this time tomorrow he would be gone and she would be alone again.

Back in the main room of the house, the men were waiting for them. Mark's shirt was too tight on Douglas across the shoulders, but that was a small thing compared to his pants. He had slit the material of the leg to fit over the cast. Mark was wearing Douglas' jeans with the ruined leg pinned together. From a distance and in the dark of night, one could easily be fooled into believing Mark was Doug... if not for the cast.

Alex bit her lip wondering if she could make Meeks ignore it. She would have to. "Okay. Is everyone ready for the show?"

"I forgot something."

Alex waited while Doug went off to get whatever he had forgotten. "I want to thank you guys for helping him like this."

Lloyd waved that away. "Wouldn't have missed this for anything."

Alison nodded.

Mark and Susan murmured something along the same lines. Just then, Douglas returned and helped lift one end of Michael's trunk. They had packed away Doug's sword with his old clothes and boots in the trunk. It hadn't been said, but no one was expecting him to return to the farm. If all went well, he would force Karel to take him home to Inari.

Michael backed out the door carrying the trunk and the others followed. The SUV was parked directly in front of the house in full view of the gate where Meeks had parked his cruiser. Alex had no doubt he could see them all in the light coming from her windows.

Doug shoved the trunk into the back of the SUV and Michael slammed the hatch closed.

Alex hustled Mark and Susan into the shadow of the vehicle ready for the switch. "When it's done, I want you to wait here to see us off. Keep in the light and wave to attract Meeks' attention. That should be enough to fix the image in his mind. When we've gone, just go back inside and make yourselves at home. Watch the television or something. Don't turn out the lights until after twelve; he knows my routine. I never go to bed before that. Okay?"

"Gotcha," Mark said. "It'll work."

Alex nodded. "Here goes."

She closed her eyes and opened herself to the web. A flood of impressions swamped her senses. Nuisance was feeling a little huffy because he hadn't been ridden today. Smokey had an itch. Michael was worried that he should have told Sandy to stay in L.A. He was feeling guilty for bringing the others too. He wished he had come alone. Alison was thinking that if they didn't get on with this, she would just scream. Lloyd was thinking about the lodestone—he wanted to do magic like that. Douglas was thinking…

Her eyes snapped open and she blushed.

Doug frowned, and she quickly closed her eyes again determined not to think about what she saw in Doug's head. He must have lowered his shields when they cast the spell and seeing herself the way he saw her was embarrassing.

Making herself concentrate on what she had to do, she followed the web to Meeks. It was an incredibly short journey. He was sitting in his car less than two hundred yards from where she was standing. He was watching the house and the SUV, but was thinking about shift change. Jenn would relieve him in an hour. She concentrated hard on the image of herself and Douglas standing outside the house waving at the SUV as it left. When she had the image perfectly formed, she thrust it into Meeks.

Alex winced as his life thread hummed discordantly in her mind. If she hadn't known it was a misuse of her power before, she did now. The discord told her the goddess would not be pleased with her. Meeks had been harmed by her use of her gift on him, though she wasn't sure how exactly. She hadn't hurt him in the traditional sense, but she had abused him. There were many kinds of harm. The discordant humming told her more clearly than anything else did, that her choice of magic over physically knocking him out was the wrong choice. She would pay for her poor judgment. Maybe not today, maybe not even this year, but she would pay. By the threefold law, she would pay.

An it harm none, do what thy will.

She had lived by the Wiccan Rede most of her life. She hadn't always been successful, but she had tried very hard, and for the most part, she had succeeded. This wasn't the first time she had deliberately influenced someone, and it probably wouldn't be the last. She felt guilty about that, and promised the goddess she would consider all other options before she did it again. That was all she could really do anyway. Causing a small hurt to avoid a bigger one sounded logical, but to the goddess, hurt was hurt. The only way to make amends was to use her gift to help not harm.

"It's done," she said. "Let's go."

Everyone climbed into the SUV. Mark whispered good luck, and with his arm around Susan, he waved as Michael started the engine and drove toward the gate. He paused to check the way was clear before pulling out onto the road.

Meeks peered into the SUV, and then turned back with a

frown on his face to watch Susan and Mark walk back to the house.

Alex watched all this with her lip between her teeth. Meeks was fighting it. He was fighting her influence. She was about to compound the misuse of her gift by pushing Meeks again, when he suddenly relaxed. Mark had disappeared back inside the house. It was the damn plaster cast. Meeks had noticed that Mark wasn't in a cast, and it conflicted with the image she had forced on him. As soon as the anomaly was out of sight, he had forgotten about it. In a couple of hours, he would remember again, and then there would be hell to pay.

"Drive fast," she said.

* * *

Tomas leaned back in his chair and stretched. His groan as muscles popped was half pleasure half pain. He had been sitting too long. He checked his watch and was surprised to find it was after ten already. He should have left the office hours ago, but there was nothing at home he needed, and there was certainly no one there that needed him.

He lived alone. No wife, no kids, no pets or family awaited him there. His life was here. Was that sad? He didn't think so, but was it? He was sure some people would think so, but he wasn't one of them. The uniform and badge he wore had always been enough for him… he frowned. When had he started lying to himself?

The badge was the most important thing in his life *now*, but it hadn't always been so. At one time, he had been like any other guy. He would spend his time dating and going out with women, well girls—it had been a long time ago and he had been no more than a kid himself. Alex had changed that, changed him really. The first time he dated her, he had known he was going to marry her. Funny how wrong people can be about things. Alex had made him swear off other girls. Not that she had said or done anything, but he hadn't wanted to risk losing her.

He stood to work the kinks out of his legs. He automatically settled his gunbelt more comfortably upon his hip as he did so. He should start jogging again, he thought. He lifted in the gym twice a week, but maybe he needed more than an upper body workout. He sucked in his burgeoning gut and held his breath. He wasn't fat, but he wasn't as trim as he had once been either. His thoughts flashed to Skeldon—the very athletic, the very trim looking Douglas Skeldon, and scowled. It annoyed him that he was comparing himself unfavourably with Doug Skeldon.

What was Skeldon to Alex really? A friend she said. A good friend. How good would that be? It wasn't as if Alex owed him an explanation, but still. When she left for L.A and her new life, he hadn't expected ever to see her again. She no doubt had made many friends there. Men friends? Some. Some of them were visiting with her right now. He had checked them out after getting their names from the hotel's register. They all seemed like nice people. Only one of them was unmarried, and Lloyd Hawkridge wasn't Alex's type.

Tomas opened a drawer in his filing cabinet and thumbed through its contents. He pulled out a report his predecessor had written then dropped it back in the drawer unread. He slammed the drawer closed and wandered his office again. He stopped at the window and peered out into the night. He could see the hotel and its parking lot clearly from here. The fancy SUV that Alex's friends had hired wasn't there. He supposed they were having a party or something at her place. He should feel pleased that she wasn't alone out there... alone with Skeldon.

He scowled.

Would Alex invite him to the wedding? Would he have to watch another man take what was his... God dammit! Alex wasn't his. She wasn't anyone's property. It was that kind of thinking that had driven her away in the first place.

"You stupid bastard," Tomas hissed with loathing for the boy he had been back then. "You stupid fool boy! Why couldn't you have pretended to understand her, why did you have to push her into proving it? Why didn't you just nod and smile and let it go?"

He sighed wearily. A relationship based on untruths and misunderstanding would have been no good. Humouring her fancies, as he would have believed them to be back then, would have pushed her away as surely as his fear of her gift had done. Why did he have to keep coming back to that night? Why did his life seem hollow when he did?

"…yeah, I'm going out there now."

He turned to the door as it opened to admit Jenn. Holding the door open, she nodded at someone in the hallway, Neil probably, and then stepped fully inside.

"Just wanted to let you know I'm off to Alex's place," Jenn said. "You want me to fill her in on the latest?"

Tomas began to nod, but then he changed his mind. "I'll come out with you. Meeks can drive me back."

Jenn nodded.

He grabbed his hat and followed Jenn out to her car.

As Jenn piloted the car through the night, he reflected upon what he had to tell Alex.

Another body had been found in Westwood. The MO was exactly the same—no eyes, no heart, runes cut into the torso. Another man this time, and they didn't have a name for him. Alex could probably have named him, but Sheriff Larson would not hear of letting *that Yorke woman* anywhere near his crime scene. He could hardly blame Larson for that feeling, but it was a damn frustrating attitude. Larson didn't know Alex, but even if he had known her, he wouldn't have invited her to take a look. He was new in the job and needed to prove himself. Bringing in *a psychic like Alex Yorke*—Larson's words—was out of the question. He would be laughed out of his job!

Tomas had some sympathy for Larson. He knew what it was like having to answer to the Mayor and Town Council. He was lucky in that Mayor Polson ruled her councillors with an iron fist, and she knew Alex was no fraud. She didn't like that knowledge, didn't personally like Alex at all, but she had made it clear to him that she supported him in whatever he deemed necessary to hunt down Sharon Brydon's killer; even if that meant using Alex's voodoo.

"So," Jenn said after ten minutes of silence. "Have you decided?"

"Decided?"

"What to tell Alex."

He shrugged. "I think the truth is best, don't you?"

"Usually is. Especially with Alex. She'll know if you lie to her."

"I know," Tomas said grimly, thinking back to that night yet again. Fool boy, he should have... to hell with it. He scowled. "I can't tell her much anyway. I don't know much!"

"Larson's still holding out on us?"

"Can't blame him I guess. He's got to make his mark."

"And meanwhile people are dying," Jenn said sourly.

"Yeah. There's nothing I can do. I can't force his cooperation. Our little deal didn't work out so well. We walked the walk and talked the talk for a while; checked out each other's evidence. It went nowhere. The Brydon girl was found on my turf, but the latest victim lived *and* died in Larson's. It doesn't take much to assume that Larson has worms in his apple barrel does it?"

Jenn snorted. "You think the one we want lives in Westwood?"

"I sure hope so. At least we'll have a chance of getting him if he's a local. God help us if he isn't. All that stuff about a shadow, and Alex's feeling the perp was hanging around to the south of town, didn't come to anything. I've had everyone beating the bushes for days and they found zip. It looks as if we're out of it. It's Larson's show now."

"Can't say that bothers me too much, Tom. The only reason for us to get involved is another body turning up around here, and it might be someone I know. I can live without that thanks very much."

"Same here," he said with a shiver.

For a time there, it had seemed that Alex might be a target, but that fear was easing somewhat now. There had been no sign that the murderer was even aware of her as a danger to him. He would like to keep it that way.

The drive was almost an hour long, and Tomas found himself nodding off. One moment they were just leaving town, the next Jenn was downshifting as she approached the Yorke Place. Jenn slowed the car when the farm came into view, and pulled up next to Meeks' cruiser.

Tomas rolled his window down. "Anything?"

Meeks shook his head. "Nothing, Sheriff. Her friends left about a half hour ago in that fancy-pants van of theirs. The lights are still on up at the house, so I guess they're watching TV or something."

Tomas nodded, but he was wondering where Alex's friends had gone. They hadn't gone back to town. Jenn would have awoken him if they had past them on the way. "Which way they headed?"

Meeks nodded up the road. "South."

"South?"

"Yup."

"Follow us up to the house," Tomas ordered and waved Jenn on through the gate. "Something doesn't smell right."

"Come on, Meeks was right on her gate. What do you think she's going to do, fly away on her broomstick?"

He made a show of checking the night sky for low flying witches. "Maybe not."

Jenn grinned. She parked the car next to Alex's beat up truck, and Tomas climbed out. Meeks' cruiser rolled up behind

Jenn. Tomas settled his gunbelt more comfortably on his hip and put on his hat. Meeks and Jenn climbed out of the cars to join him, and together they surveyed the yard and house for anything amiss. It was a reflex action.

All was quiet. The barn and paddock were lost to the night, but the house was another matter. Alex hadn't gone to bed yet. Her drapes were still drawn and the yard was lit from the light pouring from the windows. The sound of a television could be faintly heard, but that was all.

Tomas led the way up the steps of the veranda. He knocked on the door and someone switched off the television. He knocked again and cocked his head at the sound of urgent whispering from within the house. No one came to answer the door. He banged on the door again, much harder this time, but there was still no answer.

"Alex?" he called loudly. "It's me, Tom. Alex?"

"...do we do now?"

"...we have to answer it..."

Tomas hammered on the door rattling it in its frame. "Police! Open up right now—*now!*"

The door finally opened to reveal a worried looking man and woman. The woman peered around the man's shoulder. Tomas didn't recognise them, but it didn't take much work to guess they were some of Alex's guests from the hotel.

"Can I come in?" Tomas said pushing past the man and into the house. "Where's Alex?"

"Ermmm," the man said looking worriedly at his wife. "She... I mean Alex is..." he clamped his lips shut looking worried.

Tomas pointed at the other doors. Jenn nodded and went to search for Alex, but Meeks was gaping at him and didn't move. "What?"

"She's right there," Meeks said pointing at the woman.

"What the hell are you talking about?" Tomas snapped and turned his anger upon Alex's guests. He didn't expect to find

Alex here, not now. "Names."

"I… we… I mean Mark. My name's Mark Noble and this is my wife Susan. We're friends of Alex."

"I guessed that," he said harshly and tried to ignore Meeks' pleading look for attention, but he couldn't. "*What?*"

Meeks shook his head. "She's right there," he said pointing at Susan again. "Can't you see? I… I don't understand."

Tomas felt his rage redden his face. "If you've been drinking on duty, so help me God, I'll—"

"Not a drop I swear!" Meeks said starting to shake. "I don't understand…" he began, but then his eyes almost bugged out of his head. "*Jesus Christ!*"

Tomas jumped forward to grab Meeks as he backed away so hard from the Nobles that he nearly fell out of the door. "Nick! What is it man, what's wrong with you?"

Jenn ran back into the room with her weapon drawn and looking for trouble.

Meeks pointed at Susan. "She changed. She wasn't her. She was Alex but now she's not!"

Tomas glared at Meeks then transferred it to Mark Noble who paled and stepped back a pace. "What did you give him?"

"Nothing!" the Nobles yelped in unison. "We didn't do it—anything."

A chill gripped him. "Where is Alex Yorke? What did she do to my deputy?"

Mark shook his head unwilling to speak.

Tomas turned back to his shaking deputy. "Are you all right now, Nick?"

Meeks nodded unsteadily. "I think so. I swear Sheriff. I swear I haven't been drinking. I kept my promise. I swear I did. When we came in, he was Skeldon and she was Yorke. *I swear it!*"

"It's okay," Tomas said trying not to shiver. "I believe you."

"You... *you do?*"

Tomas knew Alex had something to do with this. She had influenced Meeks somehow, made him think she and Skeldon were still here at the farm. He remembered her trying to explain her gift to him all those years ago. She had *pushed* Meeks. That's what she called it. Pushing.

"Go out to the car and get on the radio. I want that SUV stopped."

Meeks nodded gratefully and went to do that. Tomas and Jenn turned to the Nobles.

"Listen Sheriff," Mark began warily. "We've done nothing wrong, you can't—"

"Nothing wrong!" Tomas roared at the top of his voice. Jenn jumped in shock and so did the Nobles. "Nothing wrong! You've scared one of my men half out of his wits with your goddamn games!"

"He's not hurt! Alex wouldn't..." Mark bit his lip. "I'm not saying anything else."

"Oh yes, I think you are. You will tell me exactly what Alex and Skeldon are doing, or I swear I'll lock you up as accessories to murder!"

"You can't do that!" Susan gasped fearfully. She glanced at her husband for reassurance. She didn't get it.

Tomas grinned. "Oh yes I can. I might not be able to make it stick, but I can make your stay here very unpleasant. You would be amazed how much paperwork there is in this kind of thing. I guess your lawyer might find out where you are in... let's say, five days?"

"Surely not," Jenn drawled. "We can do better than that, Tom. Remember that guy I had up for DUI? Two weeks I had him on ice. Scared him out of drinking anything for months."

Susan swallowed nervously. "Mark? They can't..."

"We don't do co-ed by the way," Jenn said. "Women's prison for you, sweets."

Susan gripped Mark's arm fearfully.

"That's enough," Mark said angrily. Jenn opened her mouth to continue her baiting. "I said quit it! You try anything against my wife, and you'll have to go through me. I'll sue you both for every fucking cent you've ever earned or dreamed of earning! That piece of tin on your chest won't save you. Do you know who I am?"

"I don't give a shit who you are," Tomas said angrily. "And I don't care who your daddy is either."

Mark's eyes widened.

"I do my homework, Mister Noble. I know who and what he is. Your daddy doesn't mean anything to me, and neither does his money and connections. Alex Yorke does. I came out here to tell her another body has been found in Westwood. She might be next."

Mark paled. "Westwood?"

Tomas growled angrily. "She's gone there hasn't she?"

Mark looked down at his wife in question and she nodded reluctantly. "She didn't go alone. She took Douglas and the others."

"Where in Westwood?"

Mark shook his head.

"Where?" he barked angrily.

"I don't know! I swear I don't know."

Jenn prodded him in the chest with a finger. "Why go there if they don't know where they're going?"

"You won't believe me," Mark said miserably and rubbed his chest.

"Try me."

Mark took a deep breath and sighed. "We, Alex and Douglas, cast a spell to help them find who they're looking for. That's why she asked us to visit. They couldn't do it alone."

"A spell," Tomas said deadpan.

Jenn looked at him in stunned amazement.

He shook his head wearily. What really worried him about

this conversation was that he wasn't freaking out. He wasn't surprised to hear that Alex was casting spells now. She had been holding out on him ever since Skeldon appeared.

"What else?" Tomas asked, wanting the worst in one jolt.

Mark sighed. "They're looking for a man called Mardus. He works for another guy called Karel. Douglas says Karel is the one who killed that girl."

"He does, does he?" Tomas said through gritted teeth. That bastard must have known from the first who the murderer was, and yet he said nothing. "What is Karel to Skeldon?"

"They're enemies. Karel and Mardus tried to kill him."

Jenn raised a sceptical eyebrow. "Let me guess, you don't know why and you don't know where they are."

Mark shook his head. "Somewhere in Westwood."

"A motel," Susan added and Jenn's look sharpened. Susan faltered under her regard. "I just remembered that. Alex said she saw Mardus in a motel after the…"

"After the spell," Jenn said not quite disbelievingly.

"Right," Susan said.

Tomas was thinking about Sheriff Larson and travel times to Westwood. "You two stay here. Don't even think of leaving without seeing me. This isn't over." He nodded at Jenn. "Let's go."

Jenn followed him out to the car.

Meeks was waiting. "I've put the word out. Nothing yet."

Tomas nodded and tried to think of a dozen things at once. "You said they left a half hour ago?"

Meeks checked his watch. "Closer to forty-five minutes now."

Tomas noted the time and rested a hand on his gun. "They won't be halfway there yet. I wish I had a helicopter."

"Why not wish for a jet why you're at it?" Jenn said. "What about calling Larson?"

"I guess I'll have to," Tomas said reluctantly. "But that doesn't mean I'm leaving it all to him. We're going after her.

You too, Nick. I'll ride with Jenn and use the radio on the way. You follow us."

* * *

14~Rune Gate

At Douglas' urging, Michael drove them to Westwood in record time. Alex used her gift to scout ahead of them, detecting other road users—including a couple of police checkpoints. Michael avoided them using other routes. When they drove into the town proper, it was Douglas' turn to guide Michael using his grip on the lodestone. Alex recognised the motel first, but the lodestone made it certain that Mardus was elsewhere.

"He's not here," Douglas said, concentrating on the stone. "Keep going this way but slowly please, Michael. He feels close."

Michael nodded and kept the speed down.

"What the hell is he doing up this late?" Alex muttered.

"Maybe he's in a bar?" Sandy said with a shrug. "Even killers must like a drink now and then."

Douglas ignored the chatter as the others discussed possibilities. He wasn't interested in possibilities at the moment. He was only interested in certainties, and Alex's magic wasn't making it easier. He said nothing. It wasn't her fault she couldn't rein in her powers, and it wasn't her fault he had lowered his shields to better sense what the lodestone was telling him. It was just the way things were.

"He's still up ahead of us," Douglas said finally, and Michael increased their speed just a little more.

Alex angled the map she was holding toward the light. "There's not much this way. It looks industrial."

"Industrial?" Douglas said.

"Like… warehouses and stuff."

He nodded thoughtfully. "Plenty of room to hide in a warehouse I expect."

Alex nodded. "We still don't know what Mardus and Karel are doing here. Maybe they need the space."

"Maybe."

Douglas had no idea what Karel's reasoning was for coming here, but that didn't matter now. The fear that Karel might make use of what he had learned was much on his mind. There were many things about Alex's world he was not comfortable with, but by far the most dangerous was science magic. It put things long withheld from the untutored into their hands. Dangerous things; things like guns. Weapons training in Inari took years, and discipline was part of that training, but put a gun in the hand of even a common thief, and he would have the advantage over the best swordsman in the land. Wallace could form an army of peasants in a matter of days. Was it only Douglas' fear that continually brought his mind back to that, or was there a real possibility that Wallace had ordered Karel to do exactly that?

"Stop here," Douglas said suddenly when he realised what the stone was trying to tell him. "He's in there."

Michael pulled over to the curb and turned the motor off. "Here, you're sure?"

Douglas nodded, there was no doubt.

"Paragon Shipping," Alex said, reading the sign above the building's main loading doors. "There's a light, someone's home."

"He's inside," Douglas said, the lodestone was certain.

Alex opened her door to let him out. Michael opened the

tailgate and Douglas retrieved his sword. Lloyd and Alison watched him don his sword belt in silence, but then asked the question he had been waiting to hear.

"Are you sure we can't help?" Lloyd said. "Maybe we should come in with you."

"I'm game," Michael said and Sandy paled.

Douglas was already shaking his head. "It's too dangerous. I can protect myself best by sneaking in. I dare not risk magic to hide us all. Karel will be sure to sense that. You should go."

"We can't just leave!" Alex protested. "I can't go without knowing if you're all right."

"Alex…" he began, but there wasn't anything he could say to make the parting easier. It was best done quickly. "Here, keep it to remember me."

Alex took the arrowhead. "Doug I—"

"I wanted to make you a ward stone as a thank you gift, Alex. I'm sorry I didn't think of it sooner. It's too late now."

Alex looked down. "I understand. You don't owe me anything."

Douglas shook his head. "I wish things might be different. I wish many things that cannot be." He leaned forward and tentatively kissed her brow. "I have to go."

"I know," Alex whispered, watching intently as he stepped back.

Douglas turned and trotted away into the shadows leaving his friends behind. He put Alex and what she had come to mean to him, firmly out of his mind and drew his sword. The warehouse was a huge menacing shadow in the darkness. The loading door was a strange thing of ribbed metal obviously made with science magic, but there was a smaller portal to one side of it that was more to his liking. It was locked. Scouting around the side of the huge building, he found nothing to help him enter, but at the back he found something unexpected— another loading door, this time open to the night and busy with men going to and fro.

He ducked back into the shadows and watched. He recognised Mardus immediately, and his grip upon his sword tightened. He would give much to confront the man, but to do so here would be foolhardy. He watched Mardus direct his men to unload something from the back of a truck. The huge man-made beast could have hauled every horse in Skeldon's stables it was so big. It wasn't carrying horseflesh this night however. He didn't know what it carried, but he didn't like the look of it at all.

Mardus wore jeans and shirt, but his men were another matter. They were alike in bearing and dress as brothers were. They were all from Inari and wearing Wallace's colours. He had seen too many men wearing that dark maroon colour to mistake it. Each man wore a white linen shirt beneath their maroon doublets and leather pants. Their feet were shod with hard-heeled riding boots that reached almost to their knees.

When the last box was unloaded and taken inside, Douglas crept forward and through the loading door. He scampered into cover before he dared to look for Mardus and Karel. The warehouse seemed even bigger now that he was inside. It was well lit with huge lamps hanging from chains anchored to roof beams of metal. More science magic. The weight of it must be staggering. America was a very rich land to use so much metal without regard for the cost. The floor of the warehouse was cluttered with stacks of crates piled high in ranks with wide aisles between. There were machines parked here and there with metal prongs on the front. He had no name for them, but he could see they were used to move crates around.

Douglas crept from one stack of crates to the next, trying to get close enough to evaluate his chances of catching Karel by surprise. That Karel had brought so many men through the rune gate was going to be awkward. He hadn't considered the possibility when he left Michael and the others behind. He could have used their help now, but he had been right to forbid them to come. Michael and Lloyd had no experience with this sort of thing.

Douglas awkwardly climbed one of the stacks cursing the cast on his leg all the way, but eventually reached the top and lay still. Down below his hiding place a space had been cleared. The boxes unloaded from the semi were stacked to one side and Mardus' men stood nervously looking at their surroundings waiting for new orders.

Mardus was talking to someone near the centre of the cleared area, but it was what lay beyond him that made Douglas tense. The grip upon his sword was so hard that he heard knuckles creak with the strain. A dead man lay upon a bloody crate with a hole in his chest where his heart should be, and beyond that a rune gate had been opened.

Douglas stared hungrily at that portal. Inari was a few short strides through that hole in reality. His flesh crawled with the magic leaking through the gate. It tasted like home. He had to get down there. He had to get down there and through the gate, but how? His hand wandered to the small of his back where Alex's gun resided. He had almost decided not to bring it; stealing from Alex felt worse than simply being discourteous to a host, but now he thanked the goddess for it. None of the men below were armed with more than a sword and dagger. No doubt, they had been brought through the gate to lift and carry those mysterious boxes. Alex's gun might be his salvation.

"Skeldon!" someone roared. "Douglas Skeldon!"

Douglas tensed and looked fearfully around. Mardus was hurrying toward something out of sight and his men had taken up guard positions. There were two men now guarding the open gate, another two remained with the boxes they had brought, while the other four were trotting after Mardus. Douglas couldn't see who or what had called him. The voice had sounded from the air itself and the echoes were disorientating. He crawled to the other side of the stack of crates, but that didn't help. He moved back to his earlier vantage and paled.

"Douglas Skeldon! I know you can hear me, my lord! I have some of your friends here with me! Come out from where you're hiding, or I will kill them one by one!"

It was Karel and he had Alex. Douglas stared at her in shock trying to think. Mardus was standing with the renegade wizard now, and looking suspiciously into the spaces between stacks of crates. Michael and Lloyd looked angry but unharmed. Sandy was obviously frightened out of her wits. She had been crying. Alex was pale but in control. He didn't know what she was feeling. Her face was completely devoid of emotion. As he focused his attention upon her, she turned a little and looked directly up at him. When she realised that she might give him away, she made herself look aside.

"Last chance, my lord!" Karel shouted. "You know I won't hesitate to make their deaths painful… in fact I'll enjoy that."

Douglas stared down at Karel with loathing. He had no choice. He had to go down there. He began to push himself up… tried to push himself up, but he couldn't move! He struggled but his body wouldn't obey him. That's when he realised what was happening. This was Alex's work. She was stopping him from coming to her aid. With that knowledge, he was able to block her influence. He slammed his shields tight against her and regained control.

"Very well!" Karel yelled and turned to Mardus. "The witch first."

"No!" Douglas screamed. "I'm coming out!"

There was a brief pause as everyone turned to look up at Douglas' hiding place.

"No tricks, my lord," Karel said.

Douglas climbed down and was forced to surrender his sword by a pair of Mardus' men. They shoved him toward Karel and the others. He tried frantically to think of some magic that would get them all out of this alive, but Karel was far superior in magic. He had been one of the Guild's most powerful runespeakers before he was made renegade by his thievery. It was hopeless.

Karel was a tall man in line with his towering reputation. He had dark hair and eyes. His beak of a nose gave him an intimidating appearance. He was wearing the robes of a Guild runespeaker, an honour he no longer deserved, but who would dare berate him?

Douglas stumbled to a halt. He glanced around at the others then back to Alex. She was remarkably calm. He could think of no reason for that. She stared at him unblinking as if trying to tell him something, but Douglas couldn't begin to guess what. Michael and the others had been separated from her and were held under guard near the bloody altar.

"Welcome, my lord," Karel said beaming a friendly smile. "It's good of you to join us."

Douglas' blood ran cold. Karel sounded completely sincere and his kindly smile seemed genuine, but Douglas knew his reputation. "I could wish for a better venue," he said sourly.

Karel laughed. "A gallows perhaps? No doubt you would prefer my execution to this."

Douglas nodded firmly.

Karel held up the lodestone. "Yours?"

He nodded and cursed silently. He had given Alex the stone not realising that Karel could track her by its link to Mardus. Of course the link would work both ways. Of course it would! Why hadn't he thought? He should have smashed the stone the moment he was done with it.

"A nice little spell," Karel mused. "Who taught it to you?"

"No one."

Karel cocked an eyebrow. "Your own design then?"

Douglas nodded again all the while trying to evaluate his chances of using his gun on Karel and his men without risking Alex. They weren't good.

"The gate... how?"

Karel beamed. "Do you like it? It's my best work. It took

years of study to create. You might say it has defined my life."
He moved toward the altar. "See this, the artefact?"

"I see it," Douglas said with distaste. Karel was obviously
very vain where his magic was concerned. Douglas was only
too happy to encourage that and play for time.

"I found this in Hardenburg." Karel stroked the hideous
thing. "The fools that rule the Guild would not heed me. They
were afraid to test its magic, but not I. I knew I was strong
enough to master it."

Douglas stared at the hideous thing where it lay upon the
corpse of one of Karel's guardsmen. No doubt, the man had
been sacrificed for some wrongdoing he had committed. The
artefact was a circular talisman. It had a hub, spokes, and rim
like a wheel, but unlike a wheel, it was carved all over with
complex runes. The Guild had branded Karel a renegade for
the attempted theft of something held in the vaults below the
Guild hall in Hardenburg... *attempted* theft. The Guild Master
had obviously lied about Karel's success, perhaps to keep the
truth from the witches.

"Let Alex go," Douglas said turning the conversation back
to the captives. "You have me. You don't need her."

"Need her?" Karel said sounding surprised. "Of course I
don't need her, but want her? Ah now, that's another thing
entirely. I've rarely felt such raw power in one so obviously
untrained in its use. I shall enjoy draining her, yes indeed.
I wonder if there are others here..." he frowned but then
shrugged. "No matter, there's plenty of time to look for them.
I'm not done with this world yet, not by a long way. It's a
fascinating place, simply fascinating."

Douglas desperately needed a distraction. Playing for time
he hoped the goddess would heed his plea and make luck bend
his way soon. "What of the others?"

Karel glanced at Michael and his friends then away,
obviously not very interested. "What of them?"

"You could let them go."

Karel snorted. "Why would I want to do that? I can't have them getting in my way, and they know too much as it is."

"They know nothing," he protested.

"They know I'm here. They know what you've told them, which I'm sure was entirely too much. I can't let them tell the authorities what they know of me. I'm sure you understand."

Douglas did, but understanding Karel's motives didn't help him. "How much is Wallace paying you?"

"Is that relevant?"

"I'll pay you to let them go and work for me instead."

Karel scowled. "Do I look like a mercenary to you?" He raised his arms theatrically so that his robes hung from his arms like wings.

Karel looked like scum to Douglas, but saying so would make things worse. "You look to me like someone in need of an honourable employer. Wallace is a traitor. Help me defeat him."

Karel sneered. "I remember honour; it's an overrated concept, and the Guild calls me traitor too, remember? I'm sure I don't need to tell you how little that concerns me."

Douglas shook his head.

"I thought not." Karel turned to Mardus. "Is everything ready?"

Mardus nodded.

"Good." Karel studied Douglas then shook his head. "I don't know why I'm bothering to ask, but... will you swear to go quietly if I promise to take you back to Inari unharmed?"

Douglas' heart skipped a beat. If he could only set foot upon Inari again, he might find a way to escape and warn the queen. He was about to agree when he remembered who he was bargaining with. "Why would you do that?" he said warily. "I oppose everything Wallace is trying to do."

Karel smiled. "Let us say that Duke Wallace and I do not see eye to eye on everything. He wants you silenced very much. He even ordered me to personally see to it. Ordered me, as if I'm just another of his lackeys! The audacity of the man is simply stunning. Suffice it to say I think it would be more entertaining if I turned you over to him."

"What about him," Douglas said, nodding at Mardus.

Karel sneered. "He will do what I tell him if he wants to live."

Douglas licked suddenly dry lips. "Swear not to kill my companions and I'll agree."

Karel shook his head. "I already told you I cannot let them loose."

"Then bring us all through the gate. What danger are they to you in Inari?"

Karel frowned and turned to assess Michael and the others. He shrugged. "None. Very well, I will bring them along."

"And Alex too!" Douglas said desperately.

"*Enough!*" Karel barked. "Do not try my patience too far. The witch is mine. I will hear no bargains where she is concerned. As for your companions, I will let them loose in Inari, but in return, you will swear not to attempt an escape. I don't care what you do after the Duke takes charge of you. Challenge him to the death for all I care. Decide now. I grow weary of talk."

Douglas turned to Alex. "I'm sorry I got you mixed up in this."

"Don't be," Alex said flicking a glance at Karel then back to Douglas. "Tomas is here."

Karel frowned. "Who is Tomas?"

Michael spoke up quickly. "I am."

"Ah!" Karel said then smiled in amusement. "You're her protector are you?"

"She's a friend of mine, yes."

"And this other?"

"My wife," Michael said.

Douglas' thoughts were racing. If Tomas was here then something might be salvaged from this mess. Tomas would not have come alone. Before he could think of what to do, Alex took matters in hand. She glared at Mardus. A second or so later, he jumped and turned at a sound only he heard.

Douglas watched in glee as Mardus made some excuse and led two of his men off to investigate. That left the two men guarding the gate, the two next to him, and another two—one each for Michael and Lloyd.

Before he could think of a way to make use of this turn of events, all hell broke loose.

* * *

15~Through the Gate

The cruiser sped through the night, sirens blaring, and flashing lights announcing its presence. Tomas was still arguing on the radio with Sheriff Larson about being included in things. The SUV that Alex's friends had hired was seen in Westwood not long ago by a patrol car heading into the Sunset Industrial Park. That alone wouldn't have raised questions, but Tomas' bulletin together with another operation in the area did raise alarms. Larson was planning to raid a warehouse in the park tonight and hadn't informed Tomas. He couldn't see how a raid on a warehouse in Westwood could have any links with the rune killer, but Alex heading into the industrial park was one hell of a coincidence. Tomas didn't trust coincidences where Alex was concerned, and Larson was being a bastard about the entire thing. Larson's lack of cooperation was telling. The raid had something to do with their rune killer, Tomas was almost sure of it. He couldn't see how, but he felt it. Larson was trying an end run around him, probably to claim all the credit. Normally that would piss him off, but he was more concerned with Alex's safety than claiming any kind of credit tonight.

"Ian…" Tomas said but Larson continued his tirade. He

tried to get a word in but then lost his temper as Larson continued his rant. "Ian!" he roared and gained a moment of stunned silence. "I don't give a fuck about your operation. Is Alex safe?"

"The Yorke woman?" Larson said after a moment of silence. He needed to change track. "I don't have her."

Tomas closed his eyes and lowered his voice, trying to sound patient. "I didn't ask that. Is she safe? Where is she?"

"How the hell should I know? Listen, Edwards. This is my operation and on my turf. I won't tolerate interference."

"I'm not interested in that. Where. Is. Alex. Yorke!" Tomas finished with a roar. Silence. "Your own men reported seeing her. Why didn't they stop her?"

"I gave orders to keep out of the area and out of sight until we've raided the warehouse. I told them to stay put, watch, and do nothing to attract attention. They did see the SUV go in, but it hasn't come out yet."

"Shit," Tomas hissed under his breath. He keyed the microphone live again. "I'm about fifteen minutes away. Wait for me."

"This is my—"

"I know and don't care. I want Alex safe, that's all."

Larson was quiet for a moment but then resumed more quietly, perhaps finally believing what Tomas had tried to say. "I heard that you and she..."

"Yeah, yeah I know what you heard, Ian. That was a while ago. We're not together anymore. I want her safe."

"Fifteen minutes," Larson said and signed off.

Tomas sighed and hung the microphone up. "Faster Jenn. We have fifteen minutes before Larson goes in. He won't wait for us."

The cruiser accelerated from dangerous to suicidal speeds. Jenn was an excellent pursuit driver. She was trained by the best, but even so, it was a scary ride. Tomas grabbed the 'oh shit' handle and held on.

"We're taking a lot for granted, Tom," Jenn said. "We don't know Alex is heading for Larson's warehouse. She could be passing through to somewhere on the far side for all we know."

Tomas shook his head. "This is Alex we're talking about. Larson is working the rune case and wants to raid a warehouse in the Sunset Industrial Park, meanwhile, Alex casts a spell to find the rune killer and is later seen entering the Sunset Industrial Park. I don't believe in coincidences where Alex is concerned, Jenn. One way or the other, I think the nightmare will be over tonight."

Jenn's lips thinned. "Yeah, this case has been one long nightmare. If we lose Alex..."

"We won't," Tomas snapped. *I won't, not again.* "We won't let anything happen to her. Just get me there before that idiot goes in with guns blazing, Jenn. Get me there and don't wreck us."

Jenn didn't answer but concentrated upon her driving. Tomas switched off the sirens and lights as they neared their destination, not wanting to queer Larson's operation and gain his ire. Nick did likewise in his cruiser following faithfully behind.

Sheriff Larson did wait to go in, but not because he was waiting for Tomas to arrive. He had his own reasons as Tomas later learned. Jenn and Nick parked their cars in the side streets away from Paragon Shipping's Westwood warehouse, and joined Larson at his command centre. Larson had chosen to use one of the industrial units on the same road as Paragon, but a few hundred yards from it. Tomas entered from the side not the front in case of watchers and found Larson leaning upon a table covered in papers surrounded by his men. Behind the sheriff, a white board had been set up with a street plan drawn upon it. Tomas gave it only a brief glance.

"Ian, a word?" Tomas said. Larson looked up and nodded.

Jenn and Neil joined Larson's men intent upon learning all

they could. Tomas and Larson stepped into an empty corner to talk in private.

"Thanks for waiting for us, Ian. Fill me in?"

Larson nodded. "Paragon Shipping, it's a warehouse a couple of units down. They tranship for a few companies here in Westwood. Legit operation I had always thought... until now."

"They're dirty?"

Larson nodded again. "We've been trying to crack a fencing ring for months now. We knew it was happening, but we couldn't find anyone willing to talk. We caught a lucky break just yesterday, and that led us here. Paragon is fronting for them, moving stolen goods using their regular shipping routes."

Tomas frowned. "Okay, but how does that connect with the rune case?"

Larson frowned. "It doesn't as far as I know. You think it does, why?"

This was going to be interesting. Larson would not believe what Tomas knew to be true regarding Alex and the casting of spells. He tried to think of a way to explain things without destroying his credibility.

"You know Alex Yorke has helped me in the past, Ian."

"I told you before what I think about that."

Tomas scowled. "I remember. Alex and some friends have taken matters into their own hands. I didn't find out until too late, but she seems to think that she knows where the rune killer is."

"Here?" Larson said incredulously. "In Westwood?"

Tomas nodded. "You said your patrol saw the SUV. If we find it, that's where the killer will be."

"If you believe the Yorke woman knows what she is doing you mean," Larson said sourly, and Tomas grimaced. "I can't deal with her right now. I have to finish up here first."

Tomas wanted to argue, but he couldn't. It was Larson's

show. In his opinion, the rune murders should have been the priority, but it wasn't his jurisdiction and the raid on Paragon would be over soon. At least, he assumed it would. It had better be soon, because Tomas had no intention of waiting until Alex dropped herself into serious trouble.

"I'll wait," Tomas said. "But not forever, Ian. This better be done with soon."

"It will be. We're waiting for them to make a final delivery before going in."

Tomas and Larson went back to join the others, but before they were even halfway across the room, Larson was called away. Tomas watched him leave to consult with one of his men, and worried about Alex. Where was she now? God, he hoped she was safe. Larson turned away from his man and Tomas' eyes connected with his. Tomas felt a thrill of fear run down his spine. Something was wrong. He hurried over to Larson.

"What's happened?" Tomas said.

"Your girl has just fucked up my day, that's what."

Tomas blinked uncertainly. "What?"

"The Yorke woman and four friends were just seen entering Paragon."

Tomas closed his eyes and shook his head. He'd known it would come to this. Known it from the first. There was a link between the rune killer and Larson's case here at Paragon, and Larson had slowed him down. He should have gone in without him, should have barged straight in and to hell with the politics of the situation. It would have blown Larson's deal here all to hell, but Alex would have arrived too late to be endangered. Now she was surely in the greatest peril imaginable.

"When do we go in?" Tomas said.

"We don't. This is a possible hostage situation now," Larson snarled.

That was the wrong decision. Tomas knew it was. He felt it was down to his toes. The rune killer was in there with Alex.

He couldn't let Larson wait.

"Are your people close enough to see what's happening inside?"

Larson nodded. "Spotters on the roofs, snipers, the works. I'll need them more than ever now. I'll get a negotiator over here."

"It won't help. The rune killer is in there. He won't negotiate."

Larson hesitated. "We don't know for sure."

"Alex knew. How do you explain it otherwise? How did she know to come here? How did she know about Paragon?"

Larson's uncertainty faded. "We go in."

Tomas nodded. "Fast and hard."

The decision made, Larson became a different man. All uncertainty gone, he gave his orders crisply and without hesitation. His men moved with speed to surround the warehouse. Larson waited just long enough to hear reports before announcing their presence.

"This is the police!" Larson began.

* * *

"This is the police!" a voice boomed. "We have the building surrounded! Drop your weapons and come out with your hands up!"

Karel's reaction was immediate. He snatched up the artefact from the cooling corpse of his guardsman and back-pedalled toward the gate dragging Alex with him. She struggled and kicked, but Karel's arm around her throat was immoveable. Before Douglas could think to intervene, they were through the gate and gone.

"Alex!" Michael shouted in dismay.

Douglas turned in a frenzy. No time, no time, no time! He had to get through before Karel closed the gate.

He punched one man full in the face with his entire body

behind the blow. He felt bones crunch under the impact and the guardsman collapsed. The other guard drew his sword and swung in a simple chop designed to take his head. Douglas threw himself flat, and rolled into the guard holding Lloyd. Both men fell. Lloyd managed to fall on top kicking and punching all the while.

Douglas caught sight of the two guards nearest the gate jumping through it followed by Mardus who was running full tilt away from someone close behind him. Douglas ripped the gun free of his waistband and still on one knee, he shot the guard fighting with Lloyd twice in the back, then fired again, this time at the guard dragging Michael like a shield toward the gate. Both guards died instantly.

All was chaos. Guardsmen ran toward the gate but were tackled by men in uniforms similar to the one Tomas wore. Sandy was shrieking at the top of her lungs. Michael was covered in blood, not his, and staring into the gate full of indecision. Lloyd had no such concern. Without a thought for the consequences, he barged past Michael and through the gate in pursuit of Alex. Alison gasped in shock and jumped after him. Douglas climbed to his feet and charged the gate fearing it would close in his face.

"Skeldon!" Tomas roared and tackled him just as he reached the gate.

Staggering and lashing out wildly, Douglas fell with Tomas clinging to his legs into numbing cold and blackness; a black void that went on forever.

* * *

16~Epilogue

Agent Freemont shook his head as he re-read Sheriff Hale's final report on the rune serial killer. It was well written, but it came across like a screenplay for HBO. Nobody really believed the killer had come from another world and escaped back to it. Laughable, except he had met the police officers who had witnessed it. Their statements all matched and face to face, they came across as reliable witnesses. The usual cover of drug ingestion or mass hallucination wouldn't work this time.

The others thought he was nuts giving them any credit, but he believed every word. They hadn't met Jenn Hale, or checked out the evidence. He had. He had visited Westwood to see the prisoners, and he knew the truth. It wasn't anything he could make the others believe, but those horrified and scared men were never born on this world. Language was an obvious tell, but it wasn't just that they didn't speak English or any other earthly language. They were like children, scared of everything. He knew people. It was part of what made him a good investigator. They were scared of everything and it was no act. Turn a light on and they flinched, make a phone call or turn on the TV and they flinched again; put them in a car for transport and they nearly fainted. They didn't belong here.

He felt sorry for them.

The rune killer had escaped. That was damn unfortunate, but they had sketches and a name for him. The case wasn't exactly closed but it was solved. Karel was now a known felon in the States as Freemont suspected he was in his own country. An illegal alien too, more alien than usually came across the borders. If he ever showed up again, he would find it much harder to move about freely. His accomplice, Mardus, was also in the files.

Sheriff Tomas Edwards, Douglas Skeldon, Alexandra Yorke, Lloyd Hawkridge, Alison Cully, Michael Norris, and Cassandra Norris were all listed as missing. Freemont hoped they were well. It was all anyone could do. He especially hoped that wherever Alex was now, she had found some peace.

As for Jenn Hale, the Mayor of Susanville promoted her to Sheriff that very night, once it became clear that the portal, gate, or whatever it was eventually called wasn't going to reopen. She was the first female Sheriff Lassen County had ever had. Privately she had told him that she was just keeping the chair warm for Sheriff Edwards, but Freemont had a feeling that she would be using his office for a long time to come. She had closed up Alex's house and sold off the animals. She took the cat home and kept the horses, but stabled them closer to town.

Paragon Shipping was dirty, just as Sheriff Larson had suspected, and its employees were currently awaiting trial. The crates and boxes piled up near the murdered man in the warehouse, turned out to contain rifles and handguns with enough ammunition to fight a small war. Larson had expected electronics like microwave ovens and DVD players not guns, and had found plenty of them in the rest of the warehouse, but he couldn't account for the weapons. There had been no indication of gun running at Paragon before. His informants denied any knowledge of such. Freemont suspected the guns were a new wrinkle, and probably linked to Karel and Mardus.

He had a feeling that Evan Currie's drug money had paid for them. Serial numbers had been removed from everything of course, and without those identifying marks, finding out where they came from would be very hard.

Freemont closed the folder and stood. He carried it to one of the battered filing cabinets. He opened the second drawer and dropped the folder inside with the others. He thumbed through them and his lips twisted. All of them were hard copies of files that were on the FBI system. He had started making backups of his strangest cases about fifteen years ago when he noticed that one of his old case files had been inexplicably edited to change certain facts. He would never have found out if he hadn't run across a new case that reminded him of an old one. When he looked back for research, he had found the details altered. Now he kept hard copy backups and digital backups on memory sticks for his own peace of mind. Would he one day look back at the rune serial on the main system to find it erased or changed? He wouldn't be at all surprised. There were agencies that did that sort of thing. Agencies with acronyms he wouldn't say aloud.

Freemont shrugged into his coat, turned off his desk lamp, and left his office. It was time to forget his worries for a few hours. He would go home and kiss his wife, and pretend serial killers from other worlds didn't exist.

* * *

Also available from Impulse

If these books are not available from your local bookshop, send this coupon together with your check made payable to:

Impulse Books UK

At the following address:

Impulse Books UK
18, Lampits Hill Avenue,
Corringham
Essex SS177NY
United Kingdom

Please send me the following great titles from Impulse Books UK

Tick as approrriate:

The God Decrees (Pb)
ISBN: 0-9545122-1-9 £8.99 _____ ☐

The Power That Binds (Pb)
ISBN: 0-9545122-2-7 £8.99 _____ ☐

The Warrior Within (Pb)
ISBN: 0-9545122-0-0 £8.99 _____ ☐

Dragon Dawn (Pb)
ISBN: 978-1-905380-02-2 £8.99 _____ ☐

Wolf's Revenge (Pb)
ISBN: 978-1-905380-43-5 £8.99 _____ ☐

NAME _____

ADDRESS _____

_____

_____

I have enclosed a check for the sum of £ _____

Please be sure to add £2.25 to your order to cover shipping and handling charges.

Also available from Impulse

If these books are not available from your local bookshop, send this coupon together with your check made payable to:

Impulse Books UK

At the following address:

Impulse Books UK
18, Lampits Hill Avenue,
Corringham
Essex SS177NY
United Kingdom

Please send me the following great titles from Impulse Books UK

Tick as approrriate:

Hard Duty (Pb)
ISBN: 978-0-9545122-3-1 £8.99 _____ ☐

What Price Honour (Pb)
ISBN: 978-0-9545122-5-5 £8.99_____ ☐

NAME _____

ADDRESS _____

_____

_____

I have enclosed a check for the sum of £ ____

Please be sure to add £2.25 to your order to cover shipping and handling charges.